abigail parker
and the *shade tree*

a story by
matthew childress

TATE PUBLISHING *&* *Enterprises*

Published by Tate Publishing & Enterprises, LLC
127 E. Trade Center Terrace | Mustang, Oklahoma 73064 USA
1.888.361.9473 | www.tatepublishing.com

Tate Publishing is committed to excellence in the publishing industry. The company reflects the philosophy established by the founders, based on Psalm 68:11,
"The Lord gave the word and great was the company of those who published it."

Book design copyright © 2007 by Tate Publishing, LLC. All rights reserved.
Cover design by Steven Jeffery
Interior design by Lindsay B. Behrens

Published in the United States of America

ISBN: 978-1-60462-452-6
1. Fiction   2. General   3. Fantasy
07.12.28

abigail parker
and the *shade tree*

This book is dedicated to my family. My wife and daughters have believed in me for many years. To Scotia, Molly, Hannah, Rebekah, and Sarah, thank you for giving me the strength and courage to follow my dream of writing. May God's blessing come your way.

Prologue

Have you ever had a day when all your mind wants to do is drift away to some far off place? Maybe it's because your mind becomes overloaded with all the pressures of life. It seems there is always homework to be done...or chores to work on...or places to be at...or juggling relationships with friends and parents. Honestly, all of that is just too much for a kid sometimes.

The mind is a terrible thing to waste on such stuff. Maybe that's why my mind drifts. In fact, my mind drifts a lot. I guess that's because I have a lot of stuff on my mind. It's not that I have a terrible family or a hard life. Often I just feel I have a lot of stuff to deal with.

One example is school! What kid likes school? Usually the only kids I know that like school are the ones who get beat up and have their lunch money stolen. My school is okay but I don't like all the work involved. There are too many tests, too much conflict, and too much pressure to succeed. Why can't I just be a kid and not be expected to learn at a level of a kid three grades ahead of me?

When I am at home I have a list of chores I must do each day. Some say that's not a bad thing as it teaches me responsibility as I grow up. To me, it's like a legalized form of child labor. What kid likes changing the cat's litter box and scooping the dog's poop out of the backyard? Another thing, I like to wear clothes but in no way does it thrill me to fold my clothes. One of my chores is to not only fold my clothes, but even all my sisters' clothes. At least I can sometimes blackmail them because I know if their underwear has stains or not.

My parents both work so we are constantly going places that I don't want to go to. Places that deal with their work. My dad, the business owner…he owns a pet shop. He sells cool animals like dogs, cats, rabbits, and fish. But he's always working and when he's not working at his store, he's going to conventions and conferences.

My mom's job is demanding also. She is a real estate agent. She is always on the go. Especially right now when, as she says, the market is booming…whatever that means.

But sometimes my parents want to take my sisters and me to a place just for fun, like a movie or dinner. Lots of times I wish they would just go without me because I would rather spend time with my friends. Speaking of my friends…talking about the pressure of good relationships…I am always being pulled one direction or the other and many times I don't know what to do because I want to please them. It seems it is so easy to make one of my friends mad at me. There is simply too much pressure.

Anyway, I guess the only way I can escape all the pressure is to allow my mind to drift to a far away place…a happy place filled with everlasting adventure to distract me from the pressures of my life.

Speaking of my life, I forgot to introduce myself. I'm sorry. My name is Abigail. Abigail Parker. I am thirteen years old. I also have a best friend. Her name is Chelsea. Chelsea and I like to sit under the old shade tree in our neighborhood and drift to a far away place together. We do this at least three times a week.

There's just something magical about that shade tree. Chelsea and I first discovered it when we went to the park for the first time. We had been playing most of the afternoon having a grand time together.

On that day we played hard and it was getting close to the time for us to start heading back to our homes. We were kicking a soccer ball to each other when Chelsea accidentally kicked it off the side of her foot and the ball rolled to the base of the tree. I jogged over to the ball to pick it up. As I was bending over to pick the ball up, I noticed a heart carved in the trunk of the tree. It was one of those hearts that says someone loves someone else. While looking at the carved image I heard the sounds of the branches blowing in the wind. You know that crackling sound of wood bending and the ruffling of the leaves. The sounds just brought a peace to my mind.

Then I slowly panned upward into the limbs. The tree was huge. I could barely see the sunshine trickle through the thick branches. All of a sudden I got that feeling inside myself like what a baby chick might get while under the wings of its mother. I had a safe and welcoming feeling. A sense that I could lay up against its trunk, relax and everything would be alright.

Chelsea called out to me, "What are you doing over there?"

After a couple of seconds that it took me to compose myself, I shouted back, "Hey Chelsea, come over here. I want to show you something."

She ran over to me and asked, "Show me what?"

"Just look for a minute at this tree. Look at its trunk. Then look through its branches. Just listen to the tree," I said to her.

After a moment of doing this Chelsea looked at me and said, "Wow! I feel like maybe we should just sit under this tree and rest for a few minutes."

I quickly replied, "Yeah, me too. It is hot today and this tree is providing lots of shade to help us cool down."

So we both just sat down next to each other, leaning our backs against the base of the trunk of the shade tree. "This is a magical tree, don't you think?" I asked Chelsea.

She answered, "It sure is. It's so peaceful here. My mind could just go off to a far place right now."

I softly replied, "Yeah, I know what you mean." Shortly afterwards I asked Chelsea, "Hey Chelsea. Have you ever been on an adventure before?"

"What do you mean, Abigail?" Chelsea responded. "Well, kind of like a trip to another country or a far away land that you know nothing about," I said back.

"Only in my mind," Chelsea said.

With a sleepy tone in my voice I said, "Yeah, me either. But I sure would love to sometime."

Chelsea with her eyes half shut said, "Maybe we could go together."

Next thing I knew we were both waking up from a nap. The comfort we received from the shade tree had put us both asleep. I glanced at my watch. It was ten minutes after the time we were given by our parents to return home.

Little did we know that we would be out later than we thought. My story is about one specific day when we daydreamed together under that old neighborhood shade tree. It seemed like any ordinary day but it sure didn't end up as one. I don't know about your daydreams, but one of ours actually became real.

The Trail

We jumped up, grabbed our soccer ball, and began walking back home. We took the same route as we always had before. The park was on the opposite side of a thick cluster of woods that separated the park from our houses. We walked a trail that went right through the woods. This trail usually saved us about ten to fifteen minutes of walking time. We liked having the trail because it allowed us to play that much longer.

As we were walking the trail, we were goofing off with each other as usual. While we were joking and laughing we heard some noise coming from the thickets off to our right. The first time we ignored the sound and kept walking. Then we heard it again. But this time it was louder. It sounded like someone or something walking on the dried out leaves lying on the ground. As we stood there trying to see into the thick brush, we thought we saw something move. Then we got real quiet and looked really hard into the brush.

I spoke to Chelsea as I looked into the brush, "I think there's something in there."

Chelsea said with a faint sound of fear, "I think so too."

Then we both saw what seemed to be a flash of white as something ran through a small opening in the brush to hide behind some laurel bushes. At that point Chelsea and I were both afraid. We didn't know what it could be. We knew it was large and had at least some white in its color. Chelsea asked, "Could it be a bear?"

I responded, "No, I don't think so. Bears do not live this close to our houses. Besides, whoever heard of a white bear?"

Chelsea quickly said, "Have you ever heard of a polar bear?"

She thought she was so smart. But I just had to ask, "In Florida?"

After a few seconds, Chelsea made the comment, "My parents read a story in our newspaper a couple of days ago about a polar bear that escaped from our local zoo." At that point we both began to walk faster.

As we walked faster we could hear the steps of that creature in the woods walking faster behind us. Then we heard a loud sound that sounded like an animal snorting.

When we heard that sound we looked at each other and at the same time yelled, "Run!"

All we could hear was the sound of our breathing and the galloping steps of something behind us. Whatever it was it had come from out of the bushes and was now running after us on the trail. In fact, the creature had gotten so close to us we could feel its breath on the back of our necks.

Neither one of us had the courage to look behind us to see what was chasing after us. All we could do was run as fast as we could and hope the creature would give up. We ran for what seemed like several minutes but I'm sure was only several seconds. Then we came upon a small opening in some blown over tree stumps. We called it our cave when we played on the trail. We looked at each other with a look in our eyes that said let's jump in our cave. So we did.

We took refuge in that small place for a few minutes trying to catch our breaths. We looked outside the opening and could not see anything. So I looked at Chelsea and bravely said, "Go out and see if it is still here."

Thinking only about my safety, she said, "Forget that! You go out."

Then I suggested, "Let's peak out together." So we creped our way out the opening of the stumps. We looked around and listened deeply. Nothing could be found, nothing seen or heard.

At that point we breathed a sigh of relief and smiled. Then as quickly as we smiled we heard the snort again and realized that something was standing on top of the tree stumps above us.

We gulped with a sense that our time had finally come. Whatever it was, it was ready to jump on us and eat us. At the same time we slowly turned our heads so that we could see what was standing above us.

When we saw it, we screamed to the top of our lungs. It was...a horse? It looked like a horse. It had the pretty markings of a painted horse. The horse had the colors of black, white, and brown. But this wasn't just any ordinary horse. This horse had a long, pointed horn on its head. I thought to myself, *Is that a unicorn? There's no way because unicorns don't exist, they're only make believe!*

Chelsea was the first to find enough courage and strength to speak. "Is that what I think it is? You know…a unicorn?" Then she continued, "Do unicorns eat people?" I just looked at her and rolled my eyes.

We both very slowly got ourselves off the ground as not to startle this beautiful creature. As we stood there in front of the unicorn, it looked straight into our eyes with a look that made us feel completely safe.

Then we watched as this most beautiful of all horses walked from the top of the tree stumps to the ground where we were standing. Not knowing what its intentions were, we were frozen with amazement.

Finally, the unicorn stood in front of us. His eyes pierced our very souls as he looked intently in our eyes. It was almost as if he was sizing us up, like he was deciding if we were the right ones. The right ones for what we were not sure about.

As he stood there gazing at us, I blurted out to Chelsea, "What do you suppose he is doing and why is he here in our little part of the woods?"

Chelsea quickly reminded me, "He's a unicorn. Unicorns are not supposed to even exist. How do I know what he's doing or why he is here in our little part of the woods."

Then, as Chelsea finished, the unicorn bowed down before us. Yes, that's right. He bowed before us. It was just like you might expect a person to bow in front of his king. As he was bowing, the unicorn looked at us as if to say, "Get on."

"Do you suppose he wants us to climb on his back and take us for a ride?" I said to Chelsea.

"Let's find out," Chelsea said back. So we both timidly climbed on the back of this unicorn. We were afraid and excited. Then he stood back up straight. He turned his head and looked at us. Then at that moment, he spread two wings that we hadn't even seen until now.

All of a sudden he began running faster than anything we had known. Like a plane going down the runway with its wings spread for takeoff, so this magnificent horse was running down the trail with his wings spread preparing to takeoff.

Off the ground he soared as we both clutched his mane with every ounce of strength we had. Through the trees and straight up into the sky he flew with the grace and agility that is only reserved for an eagle.

This was the start of a great adventure. An adventure we could have only dreamed about under that old shade tree in the park. But this adventure was a real adventure. At that point we could only imagine what kind of adventure was ahead of us.

The Flight

We climbed higher and higher until the houses below looked like small pieces of a pop-up book. Then the unicorn hovered in mid air while flapping its wings and turned to look at both of us.

It was that same look as before except this time we both got the sense he was attempting to warn us. Our hands gripped his mane just a little harder as we both prepared for a fast flight. Then, the unicorn turned to look forward. At that point, he jetted ahead like a bullet from a gun.

We both screamed from the top of our lungs. I cannot describe the feelings of fear and excitement we were experiencing. In a matter of just seconds we were through, and above the clouds. Which direction we were heading neither one of us could figure out. While up there we felt like we were alone literally on top of the world. We were speechless. We were breathless. We were completely amazed at the beauty and wonder of the space around us.

I can remember watching the old Superman movies with my family and wondering what it would be like to fly. At that point I knew. I felt like someone had poured a bottle of freedom all over me. All my cares and pressures were suddenly gone.

Looking ahead of us we noticed a thick batch of dark gray clouds. It seemed the unicorn was flying directly to these clouds. Neither Chelsea nor I liked the looks of those clouds. We got closer and closer. I leaned forward the best I could and asked Chelsea, "Do you think he's going to fly in that gray bunch of clouds?"

"I certainly hope not," Chelsea gingerly said.

It was obvious now he was heading to those clouds. We were fifty yards away...forty yards away...thirty...twenty...ten. Then into the dark mass we went. It was like a dense fog you might see late at night while driving in the country. It was thick enough that we literally could not see five yards ahead of us.

The further we went into the clouds the colder it seemed to get. Chelsea and I literally began to shake because of the frigid air. We knew it had to be getting real cold when we began to see our breath.

Just when we thought we could not stand the cold or darkness any longer, we burst through the gray mass and into a bright light. The light was so bright it hurt our eyes. It was like going from a dark, chilly room immediately to the bright sunshine.

We looked behind us and saw the gray mass of clouds getting smaller and smaller as we flew further away from it. I turned to Chelsea as she was still looking at the clouds behind us and said, "I think we are finally out of those clouds."

She smiled at me and said with excitement, "And can you feel it, warmer air again!" She was right! The further we flew the warmer it became.

At that moment the unicorn began to descend. Then we burst through the bottom edge of the clouds. We both looked up and watched as the clouds were getting further away from us.

It was obvious the unicorn was taking us back to the ground. I don't know about Chelsea but I could not help but wonder where he was taking us. Everything seemed normal from what I could see. There were trees, mountains, rivers, lakes, and open fields. The only problem was that we lived in Florida where there were no mountains or rivers and only a few trees.

We definitely were not in Florida anymore. As we flew closer to the ground, we noticed that the mountain range was huge. We saw towering mountains with lots of rocks and lots of grass, shrubs, and trees.

Then, without warning, the unicorn nosedived straight down. It seemed he was heading on a collision course with the ground. Chelsea began to scream. I began to scream. Then out of pure panic I started to scream at the unicorn and pull on his mane. I was attempting to get him to pull up, but nothing worked.

We were quickly getting closer to the ground. Down, down, down we went. Chelsea grabbed the unicorn's neck to hold on and I grabbed Chelsea. She squeezed tighter and tighter and I squeezed her tighter and tighter. We both closed our eyes in anticipation of crashing. Just when we thought we were going to hit the ground he pulled up and flew along its surface.

After a few moments of flight along the ground he landed in a clearing in the same manner as when he took off. After he stopped running he turned his head and looked at us as if to say, "We're here."

We both dismounted from the unicorn. We gave each other a big hug of relief and laughed with joy. "We made it!" Chelsea said.

I responded by shouting, "What a ride!"

During our moment of relief and joy we noticed we were not alone with the unicorn in the field anymore. We were surrounded by small, blue, hairy creatures. They each had a weapon and were pointing their weapons at the two of us. "Where are we?" Chelsea asked me.

I said with fear, "I have no idea. But something tells me we are far away from home."

The Cave

As I looked around the field I saw more and more of these creatures. There must have been a hundred or more. Each one was between two to three feet tall. They had a round nose with solid yellow eyes and teeth hanging out their mouths.

They were, as best I could tell, covered in long, blue hair. Their long hair made me think of Cookie Monster. It was so long that some of the creatures' hair was matted, kind of like a dog. But others seemed cleaner and the wind blew their hair around like a little girl's hair on a windy, summer day.

Each of them wore different kinds of garments. Some wore potato sack looking shirts with strange markings on them. Some wore Tarzan like bottoms. Still others wore robes.

Their weapons looked like glorified spears. Each weapon had a pointed head of stone on the end of a big stick. They looked almost primal, but very intimidating. Their spear heads glistened in the light of the sun and with all of their weapons shining so bright it made them look a lot bigger than they truly were.

Then as Chelsea and I were looking at them all, one of them next to us made an attempt to communicate with us. He made a sound we had never heard before. But the funniest thing happened. The unicorn started moving its head up and down as if it was communicating back to the creature. The creature wasn't speaking to us but to the unicorn.

Then, the creature looked at us for a few seconds with a look of apprehension. "So you are the child?" the creature said to me. Both Chelsea and I were so amazed that neither of us knew how to respond. After a few seconds, the creature once again asked, "Are you the child?"

Finally I mustered up enough strength to respond, "I am a child if that's what you mean, a human child. Well, maybe not a total child. You see, I am thirteen years old. Not really a child but I guess I'm not an adult either. I don't really know what I am. I'm kind of in between life stages right now."

Then the creature interrupted me at that point and said, "I can tell by how you talk that you are who we have been waiting for."

I looked at Chelsea with a confused expression on my face. Chelsea looked back at me and shrugged her shoulders as if to say, "I have no clue what the creature is talking about."

Then the creature said to me, "I see that the unicorn brought with you a friend. She seems to be a child also."

Chelsea quickly blurted, "Like Abigail said, I'm not a child, sort of."

The creature stopped Chelsea at that point and asked her, "What is your name human child?"

She stuttered, "Chelsea, my name is Chelsea Johnson."

"The unicorn was just supposed to bring us the child we have been waiting for. However, she may need some help. So you may come with us," the creature said.

"With us? What do you mean with us? Where are we going? What are you planning to do with us?" I asked the creature.

He responded, "Please, all your questions will be answered soon enough. Just come with us for now."

At that point all the creatures pointed their weapons a little closer to us as if to move us along. The creature who spoke with us began to walk away and we began to follow. We noticed that the unicorn walked behind us and all the creatures began to make a line behind the unicorn. We had no clue where they were taking us or what was going to happen to us. All I hoped for was that we didn't end up on their dinner menu.

We quickly exited the field and began a long hike through the wilderness. It was quite beautiful, almost peaceful. No one talked or even muttered a noise. Chelsea and I didn't even communicate. I think we were so over-whelmed by everything that was happening that we couldn't open our mouths.

After a while of walking in the wilderness we heard a loud noise coming from behind a large rock. The creature leading us raised his hand and signaled for other creatures to check it out. What seemed like a dozen of them made two groups and went around the rock on both sides. They all went out of sight and then we heard this loud roar. It was so loud that it hurt Chelsea's and my ears. Then we heard the struggle of the blue creatures attempting to contain whatever was behind that rock. Then, one creature after another was thrown over the rock and each landed around our feet, alive but dazed.

Then we hear growling as the thing from behind the rock appeared. It was a massive creature. It looked similar to a bear but was about twice as big as any bear I had ever seen. It had long claws and many sharp teeth. It began to walk closer to us. All of the blue creatures were frozen. I wanted to run for my life but for some reason I thought of the instructions I had heard from my parents about how I shouldn't run if a bear approaches because that would cause the beast to chase you down. So I stood still just like the blue creatures. I looked at Chelsea and she was on her knees praying.

The bear-like thing stood before us within touching distance. It reared up as if it was going to strike us all dead and roared with the loudest sound. Just when I thought my life was over, the blue creature that was leading us reached up and began tickling the massive beast on its belly. The beast quickly lowered itself and began laughing like that of a child being tickled by its parent. I began to smile and thought to myself, *What kind of beast is this? It's not vicious at all. It's like an oversized teddy bear.*

The beast then said to the blue creature, "Okay, okay, okay, stop. I give up!" Chelsea began laughing. So did the blue creatures around us. The lead blue creature who was tickling the beast stopped and helped the beast to its feet. Then the blue creature said, "Abigail, Chelsea, I would like to introduce to you the fiercest, most vicious beast this side of the Crystal Sea. This is Tabukoo."

The blue creature then asked Tabukoo, "What are you trying to do. Scare the poor children to death? And why are throwing my soldiers around?"

Tabukoo replied, "I heard you were receiving the child today. So I wanted to give her a clear welcome to the living forest. Plus, I thought by playing rough like in our simulated games, she would be impressed by my ferociousness." Then Tabukoo looked at Chelsea and me and said with joy, "Welcome to our humble home. We forest creatures have been waiting a long time for you to show up to help us."

I spoke back, "Help you? What exactly do you mean? How can either one of us little girls help all of you?"

"You mean you haven't told her yet?" Tabukoo asked the blue creature.

"Not yet!" the blue creature said back. "It is for our leader to tell her, not me. And if you know what is good for you, you will not say anymore." Tabukoo nodded in response. "Let's get back on our journey because we still have a little ways to go," the blue creature said. So we all began the journey again. As we walked by Tabukoo, he looked at us, smiled, and waved good-bye.

It seemed we had been walking for a long time when we finally approached our destination. "Here we are. Home," said the blue creature. We stood in front of a dark cave.

I thought to myself. *What, this is home.* But I felt like all day nothing had been what it had seemed, so I was willing to give it a chance and see what was inside.

We entered the cave and as we did both Chelsea and I noticed the walls of the cave. They were covered in precious stones and other minerals, like diamonds, gold, and rubies. Our mouths dropped open in shock. I thought to myself about how rich I would be if I had just a few stones from this cave. They were beautiful. The cave was lit up from the sun shining on the stones at the opening of the cave and that light reflecting on the stones further in the cave. It was like a chain reaction that carried the sun's light deep inside the cave.

We finally began getting to a depth in the cave where the light from the stones could not keep the cave lit up anymore. At that point there were torches lit to give us light. I wondered if we were ever going to stop. Then, the blue creature leading us held up one of his arms and said, "Stop!" The blue creature turned to us and said, "You have been brought to our home. The reason is our leader desires to speak with you. But before you speak with our leader, I must tell you a few things. First, through that passage in front of us is where our leader is waiting. In order to greet our leader you must first wash your hands in our bowl at the entrance to the passage. Then you must chant three times, 'The leader is good.' Finally, you must make the terrifying sound of a croaksnakle."

I looked at the creature and asked, "What's a croaksnakle?"

The creature responded, "A croaksnakle is a terrifying animal that lives in the Crystal Sea. It is large and loves to eat anything it can catch. When it is nearby you can hear the sound it makes." Then the creature made the sound. It was definitely scary.

The blue creature led Chelsea and me to the bowl to wash our hands. As we looked in the bowl, we saw all kinds of disgusting things crawling in the bowl. There were creatures that looked like slimy worms but with horns. I saw creepy, crawly critters that reminded me of roaches but with pinchers and hair. The bowl was full of a paste-like substance. Chelsea and I looked at each other. "Gross," Chelsea said.

"Yeah. Yuck," I noxiously said. But we both did it. We stuck our hands in the goop as we were told.

After wiping our hands on some leaves lying next to the bowl, we both chanted, "The leader is good. The leader is good. The leader is good." Finally, we both at the same time did our imitations of a croaksnakle. Our sounds must not have been that good because the blue creature began to laugh but caught himself before he laughed too loud. "Very good, human children," the blue creature told us. "Now follow me and we may enter the passage to greet our leader."

We entered the passage together. The blue creature led the way, then I followed, and Chelsea brought up the rear. It was a small and very narrow fit. It got darker and darker until we could not see. I reached out in front of me to touch the creature for assurance but I could not feel him.

Then I called out for him, "Are you still in front of me?" There was no answer.

Chelsea quickly asked, "What's the matter? Please tell me that blue thing is in front of you!"

"Nope!" I said back.

"What do we do now, Abigail?" Chelsea asked me.

I said the first thing that came to my mind. "Let's keep going."

After a short time we could begin to see a light at the end of the passage. The closer we got the brighter the light became. Then we reached the end of the passage. It was a big open room and it was brightly lit by the stones that we saw when we first entered the cave.

As we scanned the room I noticed markings on the wall. The markings looked very interesting so I moved closer to them in order to get a better look. There seemed to be something familiar about the drawings. They almost appeared like a picture of a human fighting a terrible looking creature. Then I looked even closer. "No way!" I said.

Chelsea asked, "What do you see?"

I motioned and replied, "Come take a look at this, Chelsea."

"It's a human. It seems that maybe there are humans here after all," Chelsea said. Then a blue creature with a mask jumped out at us scaring us to death. Then he ran around the room angrily asking who we were and why were we in his room.

We both ducked our heads and bowed on the floor in fright. "Please don't hurt us, mister leader, "Chelsea said. "We only came to the room because we were led here by one of your servants." As Chelsea was speaking I watched the creature as he moved around. I recognized him. I just knew it had to be the same creature that led us to the room.

Then I stood and said, "Wait a minute. Aren't you the same creature that led us to this place? You look very familiar to me. You even smell familiar."

The creature stopped running around and looked at me. Then he took his mask off and said, "Very good, Abigail. Now I know you can do what you have been brought here to do."

"What do you mean by that? Brought here for what?" I asked. I was not prepared for what I was about to hear. What the blue creature was about to tell me would shake me to my bones.

The Story

The blue creature said, "First, let me tell you who I am. My name is Valcor and I am the leader of the forest creatures who have escorted you to this place. We are Hubearians and we are the guardians of the living forest to the east of the Crystal Sea."

"Hubearians? Crystal Sea?" I questioned.

Chelsea joined in, "Guardians?"

Valcor answered, "Yes. All those things."

Questions quickly filled my head. I had so many questions that they just began coming out my mouth. "Where are we? Why are we here? Why did you bring us to this cave and in this room? Why did you pretend to be taking us to your leader when you were the leader the whole time?"

Valcor said, "All your questions will be answered in due time. Let me first answer your last question. All that you have been put through up to this point was designed to test you. The rules tested your ability to follow rules. Guess what? You passed."

"Great," said Chelsea sarcastically.

"In our land it is important to follow the rules because there is so much danger around us. Especially for the both of you since neither of you know anything about this land," said Valcor.

Valcor went on to say, "Now let's talk about the wall drawings you were looking at. You are correct. There has been a human here before. It was a long time ago. A man. His name was Jonathan Parker." At that moment my eyes must have looked big as I recognized that name. Valcor continued, "That's right, Abigail. That man had your last name. In fact, that man was your great grandfather. And he was a hero."

I interrupted by asking, "My great grandfather? How did? Why was? What happened? I don't understand."

Valcor filled us in when he said, "Your great grandfather, Jonathan, was a hero to my people and all who live for good here in the land of the Crystal Sea. Sit down and let me get you something to drink and I will tell you the story."

After getting us a drink, Valcor began, "The land of the Crystal Sea has been in existence longer than any of us know. But through generations of Hubearians, we know this land hasn't always been as my generation knows it. The Creator made all of this a perfect place in the beginning. There used to be no death and no disease. There used to be no seasons, just one comfortable season all the time. We Hubearians at one time were the caretakers of all of the Creator's creation. We tended to the gardens. We took care of the animals, organized parties for all of the different creatures in the land of the Crystal Sea, and made sure nothing disturbed the harmony that we enjoyed. Then one day as we Hubearians were tending to our daily responsibilities, two humans were seen walking through an open field. It was the same field where the unicorn brought the both of you. The Hubearian leader of that generation quickly gathered his best soldiers and confronted the two humans, bringing them to the vary cave in which you sit today. Legend has it that both humans had been brought to this land by a tornado, dropping them both in the field.

"The Hubearian leader accepted the two humans as friends and taught them all he could about the land of the Crystal Sea. In turn, the humans shared all they knew about survival, technology, and creation with all of us. Soon we could do things and build things like never before. All of creation began to worship these humans. They accepted the worship. At some point they instituted a system that called for the both of them to be treated like the Creator Himself. Creatures from all around the land would bring them precious stones, build them lodging, and take care of their every need. Both of these humans stayed in our land for a long time. However, the longer they stayed, the more things around here began to change. The humans were not perfect like this land was at the time. Their corrupt nature slowly influenced creatures here. Soon, what the Creator had made so beautiful and perfect had turned to imperfection. The Hubearians and other creatures of this land began to show self-centeredness and greed. As each generation of creatures was born, so their self-centeredness and greed increased.

"The two humans could see that they were having a bad influence on all of the Crystal Sea. They discussed what they could do to help return things the way they were before they arrived. One wanted to find a way to return to where they came from thinking that if they left their presence could no longer influence the land in a negative way. However, the other human liked his position of power. He didn't want to leave at all. He desired to continue living here and eventually wanted to be leader of all creation here.

"The two humans' disagreement led to an argument and separation. The one human who wanted to stay chose to move to the other side of the Crystal Sea. The one human who wanted to leave decided to continue living with us until he could figure out a way back home.

"The human who wanted to return to his home was your great grandfather, Jonathan Parker. Each day after their split, Jonathan worked very hard to correct things in our land. He taught all of us how to love each other again. He showed us the importance of serving each other instead of ourselves. He often asked our forgiveness for what he had done and admitted his wrong doings.

"But each day the other human across the sea was growing in his selfishness. He would think of ways he could rule our land. He was able to convince all of the creatures on that side of the sea to follow his ideas of dominance. All of those many, many years of our work to preserve the harmony of the Crystal Sea had been destroyed. Soon, it became a we versus them mentality in our land. Often your great grandfather would attempt to reconcile with the other human but the other human would have nothing to do with it.

"There is one important thing that the both of you human girls need to know right now. There is a terrible side affect in this land that apparently only effects humans. You humans become what your heart is. The other human across the sea grew greedier and angrier. As he grew greedier and angrier he transformed into a hideous beast. He became a beast that desired nothing but power and pleasure at the cost of anyone who would stand in his way.

"This beast began using magic to bully different creatures into following him. Soon his magic became very strong and it brought a heavy darkness over our land. Your great grandfather was very saddened by what was happening because he felt partly responsible. Through your great grandfather's intense studying of the laws of our land, he was able to discover a magic that he thought would be strong enough to stop this evil beast. Jonathan discovered that the Crystal Sea has a power of its own. The Creator of this land gave the Sea an ability to take away any power from any creature, good or bad, if that power was used while that creature was in the water. All Jonathan needed to do was get the beast into the Sea and attempt to use its magic and the Sea would take it away.

"Your great grandfather challenged the beast to a fight. It was a fight that could include a spear or sword but no magic. The beast agreed and they met at the edge of the Crystal Sea."

I quickly asked, "Is the drawing on this wall a picture of that fight?"

Valcor responded, "Yes, it is. That battle lasted for many hours. There were times when your great grandfather almost lost his life. But he managed to survive the strength and skills of the great beast. After many hours of battle your great grandfather was able to get the beast into the Sea. At that point Jonathan challenged the beast to use his magic. At first the beast refused. But your great grandfather continued to challenge the beast to use his magic until the beast gave in. The beast attempted to destroy your great grandfather with his magic. As soon as he did, his magic disappeared forever. With the beast's guard down, the Hubearians of that day jumped on the beast, subduing it. The Hubearians used a thick net to capture the beast by throwing it over him. Then they wrapped the net tightly around the beast and drug him to the most northern part of our land where it stays extremely cold. While there the Hubearians were able to put the beast inside a giant piece of ice where the beast remains frozen to this day. But that's not the end of the story," said Valcor.

Chelsea quickly asked, "There's more?"

Valcor responded, "Yes, and this part of the story is extremely important so listen carefully." We both then looked at Valcor intently, hanging on with anticipation to what he had to say next.

Valcor continued, "Even though the beast was frozen in a big block of ice he still remains alive to this very day. He is in a frozen state of consciousness but very much alive. When your great grandfather was planning how to defeat the beast he realized that the curse that his best friend had brought on himself could not be reversed. The only way your great grandfather's best friend could be released of the curse was to be killed. Your great grandfather could not do this. He just could not bring himself to kill his friend so he decided to capture him and freeze him hoping that would put an end to all the evil of our land. Once the beast was frozen in the ice, your great grandfather attempted to bring peace back to our land by bringing the creatures west of the Crystal Sea to a peace meeting with all of us here in the living forest. Both groups signed a peace treaty and we thought that things were on their way to getting better.

"Because of our feeling of better times, your great grandfather began studying our laws to find a way back to his land. He discovered that there is a portal that connects our land to his land but it is only open high in our sky and only when the sky turns gray in one spot over the field where you arrived. Next he had to find a way to reach the portal. That's when the same unicorn who brought the both of you to us, volunteered to take your great grandfather back through the portal. So he watched the sky intently for many weeks until he finally saw the gray cloud appear. Very quickly your great grandfather jumped on the back of the unicorn and they took off for the portal. That was the last we saw of him. We know he made it back home because the unicorn told us but we do miss him.

"Your great grandfather did a lot for our land but his love for his friend prevented him from doing what needed to be done. After he left our land the creatures on the western side of the Crystal Sea began stirring up trouble again and have attempted many times to free the beast from his frozen state. We have been able to prevent them from reaching the beast but it is just a matter of time before they do it.

"Let me tell you one more thing that you must know. Our land's laws contain a prophecy that predicted all of this that has happened. The prophecy also speaks of the release of the beast to terrorize our land once again, but this time he will be even stronger and angrier than before. The beast will destroy many lives and bring destruction and evil to our land like we have never experienced before. One more thing the prophecy teaches is this. Listen please, Abigail, because what I am about to tell you is the only thing that gives all of us who desire peace, hope to carry on. The prophecy tells us that the beast will eventually be destroyed and peace will once again return to our land. However, the beast will be destroyed by a relative of the human who imprisoned the beast in the ice."

At that point I stopped Valcor and asked, "Wait. Are you saying that since my great grandfather did not kill the beast that someone else from my family will have to do it?"

Valcor said, "Yes! But not just anyone from your family. The prophecy teaches that it will be the first female born from the bloodline of your great grandfather."

Once again I stopped Valcor. "Let me think for a minute," I said. "Let me think about my family history. My great grandfather had two sons and no daughters. Each of those sons had a total of three children. All of them were boys. Wow! I never really thought about how there have been all boys in my family like that. My dad is the oldest of those three sons. I was the first girl born in our family in four generations. That's pretty cool…wait a moment. Are you saying that I am the one the prophecy speaks of?"

Valcor said, "It is you indeed."

I was speechless for what seemed like an hour. Then I mustered the strength to say, "There has to be a mistake. I am only thirteen years old and I am just a girl, not even an adult. Plus, I can't kill an insect let alone some hideous beast that your prophecy speaks of. You must have the wrong person!"

Valcor then responded, "There is no mistake. The prophecy speaks of the one who will kill the beast and restore peace to our land as the first female born in the bloodline of the one who imprisoned the beast in the ice. That one was your great grandfather and you are the first female born in his bloodline. There is no question you are the one our prophecy speaks of. We have been able to watch your family since the return of your great grandfather. Since the unicorn returned your great grandfather, the unicorn has been a spy returning to your land frequently to watch the births of your family. If you remember, each of your family's generations have been collecting unicorns. Doesn't your house have many unicorns throughout the house and don't you even collect stuffed unicorns?"

"Well yes, I do, and so has my family. So you are telling me my family's taste of collecting unicorns comes from my great grandfather's experience here?"

Valcor said, "Yes. We have sent the unicorn to each generation of your family to monitor the births of their children in hopes of discovering the one who will help us. When you were born we rejoiced for weeks. We have been waiting for the right time to bring you here to help us. Now, Abigail, is the right time."

I began sputtering, "But I can't do something as big as this. I can't fight. I'm not strong. I don't have the ability to lead others into battle. I just can't do what you are asking."

As I began to cry Valcor gently grabbed my hand and attempted to comfort me when he said, "Abigail, this calling is not about your abilities. The Creator knew from the beginning all that would happen and chose you to fulfill this prophecy. You can do what is needed of you because it is already been written out in the prophecy. Take comfort in knowing that the victory has already been won. All you have to do is be faithful to your calling and believe you can do it. As for the details of how to defeat the beast, take them one at a time."

I lifted my head with a little bit of confidence after hearing what Valcor had to say to me. Maybe what he said was true because why else would so many put their trust in a thirteen-year-old girl from Florida? "Where do we begin?" I asked Valcor.

He softly said, "We begin with your training."

The Training

As the sun rose on the next day, Chelsea and I were soundly sleeping when the sound of clashing wood woke us. With sleepy eyes we slowly sat up from the rocky cave floor where we had been sleeping. As we looked at each other we continued to hear the sounds of wood banging against each other, so we decided to get up and walk towards the sounds.

The sounds led us to the opening of the cave we had spent the night. As we walked out of the cave and onto the rocks that served as an entrance to the cave, we saw what seemed like hundreds of Hubearians practicing a fighting technique with wooden staffs. Everywhere we looked we saw pairs of Hubearians engaging each other. One would practice moves with their staff and then the other would practice moves. We could tell that they were careful not to injure each other but did push each other to learn the moves they were practicing.

At that point Valcor walked over to us and said, "Good morning, sleepy heads. I see that the sound of our daily staff practice woke you up. That's good because the both of you need to begin your training today and learning how to use staffs is where we will begin that training."

We followed Valcor to a location that had what seemed like hundreds of staffs resting along a rock wall. "Choose your staff well," Valcor instructed, "because your staff will soon become a great ally for you as you engage your enemy."

Chelsea and I looked at each other with looks of confusion and then looked at all the staffs. Chelsea questioned, "Wonder what he means by choosing our staff well? They all look the same to me."

I said, "I don't know, Chelsea. Perhaps we just need to take our time, look at the staffs closely, and pick according to our conscience."

We methodically walked by each staff looking each one over to try to get a sense which one would be best for each of us. Each staff stood around six feet tall and seemed to be about five inches thick. No doubt the staffs looked big and heavy to us. However, we did as Valcor directed remembering his emphasis on following directions. This was one of those times where we had to trust what he said even though we had no clue what was happening.

After many minutes of examining the staffs, both Chelsea and I finally picked a staff for each of us. Chelsea reached for a nice looking staff. It was faded in its color with dark knots of wood throughout the staff. As she grabbed it with her hand and pulled it to her body, we heard a muffled voice. Kind of like the sound you might hear when you place your hand over the mouth of another person when they are talking. Chelsea began screaming and threw the staff to the ground because she could feel lips moving inside her hand. She thought it might be some type of bug and she hates bugs. When the staff hit the ground we heard someone say, "Hey, why did you do that?" We didn't know where the voice was coming from and we looked all around us. The voice then continued, "I'm speaking from down here on the ground."

We looked at the staff that Chelsea had thrown down on the ground. In amazement we saw that the staff had a face and could actually speak. "Yes, it's me. I am the staff you picked. You act like you've never seen a talking piece of wood before."

Valcor jumped in, "Well, technically, these humans haven't ever seen a talking piece of wood. They come from a land where the wood can't speak."

The staff said, "That's just horrible. Wood that can't talk. Your land must be a terrible place to live in. I bet the next thing you're going to tell me is that in your land the bushes can't run either."

Chelsea and I just looked at each other with a look on our faces that said, "Uh, yeah."

The staff said, "Are you going to just let me lay here on the ground all day or are you going to pick me up? But this time don't cover my mouth so I can breathe." Chelsea slowly bent over and carefully picked up the staff. Surprisingly the staff was very lightweight and seemed to grab hold of the inside of her hand as she held on the staff. The longer she held the staff the more comfortable the staff felt. In a matter of seconds she was swinging the staff like she had been practicing for weeks.

Then Valcor told us, "Your staff, once chosen by you, will become your most trustworthy friend. It will constantly speak to you, teaching you the moves you need to know to use it in combat. This is how Chelsea can use the staff so effectively so quickly. The staff is moving for her. You will find that your staff will protect you at the cost of its own life. It will always tell you the truth when speaking to you. Your staff will always have your best interest as its top priority. Now, Abigail. Chelsea has chosen her staff. Look carefully and chose your staff."

Once again I scanned the staffs but this time I had a different perspective as I looked at them. Chelsea's choosing of her staff first had given me a sense of urgency to choose wisely. As I looked at the staffs my conscience and eyes fell on one specific staff. It was not only a beautiful staff but a very strong looking staff. The staff was dark in appearance with no blemishes anywhere on its surface. As I looked at the staff I felt like the staff was calling to me telling me to pick it because it would help me fulfill my calling and would not leave my side.

I walked over to the staff and carefully grabbed it with my hand. As soon as I held it the staff excitedly said, "Great choice, young warrior!" A smile came across my face as I instantly felt a connection with this staff like I had never felt with anyone or anything before. Even with my best of friends, Chelsea, I did not feel the closeness that I quickly felt with my staff.

I spoke up and said, "My name is Abigail. What is your name?"

My staff responded, "My name is Rod. And I am here to serve you with every ounce of my being. You, Abigail, are the chosen one to rescue my land from the presence of evil that has plagued us for a long time. You can count on me to help you accomplish your mission. You are special and a wonderful creation of the Creator. He loves you very much and has your days in his hands."

After listening to my staff I couldn't help but feel so much better about myself and what I was supposed to do. The staff's words brought confidence and boosted my self esteem. Everything the staff said just confirmed I needed to do what I was called to do. The staff seemed to confirm the Creator's hand was on me and was giving me the tools I needed to do the right thing.

Immediately the staff began moving my arm and thrusting itself in the air, allowing me to make moves with it like I could only dream about by watching some kung-fu movie back on my television in my bedroom. As we moved together it seemed like we were in slow motion because I could follow the moves very clearly. It was like the staff was communicating to my brain to move as it wanted to.

"Holy cow!" said Chelsea. "You are the chosen one," she said with amazement.

Valcor jumped in and said, "That's what I have been telling the both of you. In this land, you can accomplish great things and there is no doubt Abigail is the one we have been waiting for."

As the staff and I were moving together all the Hubearians stopped their training and gathered around us, watching intently. The staff and I were moving with confidence as if we had been in training for years. The moves we were making together far surpassed even many of the Hubearians who had been training all their lives.

Valcor grabbed his staff and jumped towards me. He challenged me by saying, "Alright, chosen one, let's see what you have." Then he thrust his staff towards my chest. But my staff moved to block Valcor and instantly we were in a training exercise. We battled for a long time. Sometimes he would get the best of me and sometimes I would get the best of him.

All the Hubearians watching were astonished that me, a little thirteen-year-old girl who had never picked up a staff, could even hang with Valcor, their best warrior. As we were training together, I got a lucky hit against him and knocked him into a bush. That move drew a bunch of gasps from the spectators. Valcor quickly got up and charged with determination to get me back. He fought hard and pressed me against a bolder. Then he looked at me with an expression that said, "I got you, little girl. Let's see what you can do now." At that moment my staff spoke to me and asked me to raise my hands with my staff in them. This would give the appearance I was submitting defeat to Valcor. So without any hesitation I did what my staff suggested. Valcor's eyes followed my hands and he began to smile thinking he had finally won. As he looked at my hands I watched his face. With his eyes focused on my hands, his smile quickly turned to a frown. Then I glanced at my hands. My staff had been raised to the top of the bolder I was pressed up against. The staff, after being raised, had rested its top against a small rock resting on top of the bolder. Then, in a flash, my staff hit the rock sending the rock towards Valcor's head. Valcor's staff reacted quickly and blocked the rock away. But the momentum of the rock hitting off the staff carried Valcor to the ground. As soon as Valcor hit the ground, I pounced over Valcor and my staff thrust itself under Valcor's chin. Valcor then smiled and said, "Okay, chosen one. You win."

I smiled and all the Hubearians began to cheer. Chelsea said, "Nice job, Abigail. You were amazing. You go, girl."

Valcor then laughingly asked, "Can I get up now?" I apologized and let him up.

We shook hands and he said, "Don't apologize, Abigail. You were training. You have quickly taken to learning how to use your staff. There is no doubt you are the chosen one and there is no shame in losing to the chosen one." Valcor, while shaking my hand, raised our hands together and turned to the Hubearians. I just stood there trying to take in all that had just happened. Needless to say I was extremely overwhelmed.

As everyone was celebrating, out of nowhere we heard a loud thud. We looked to our left and noticed that a Hubearian was lying on the ground, dead. A rock had somehow fallen on him. Then we heard more loud thuds around us. We looked up in the sky and saw large birds carrying the rocks in their talons. "We're under attack! Find shelter quick!" yelled one of the Hubearians.

There seemed to be more birds in the air than I could count. These were not just ordinary birds. They were black and green in color and were bigger than any birds that I had ever seen. Their beaks and talons looked like weapons ready to tear apart any flesh they could get a hold of.

Valcor grabbed Chelsea and me and told us to follow him. We ran with all our strength. Rocks were landing all around us, occasionally hitting Hubearians in the process. We were heading for the caves when I looked up and saw a rock heading right for me. As the rock came closer and was about to slam into my head, my staff instantly raised itself in my hands and blocked the rock. But the tremendous power of the falling rock knocked me to the ground, separating my staff from me. Rocks were dropping everywhere. I knew I had to get up and take my staff to safety. There was no way, after becoming attached to my staff, I was going to allow my staff to lay out there defenseless and get crushed. I rolled towards my staff, just missing a rock that landed where I was lying. I placed my hand on my staff and jumped up. Once again we headed for the cave. My staff was blocking rocks that I did not even see coming. As we drew near to the cave, a large rock fell from the sky and trapped me in a circle of rocks. Rocks were falling and I only had one chance to escape. Somehow I had to get over the large rock in front of me. My staff spoke to me again with an idea. My staff said, "Run! Run as fast as you can straight toward the rock." So I again trusted my staff, knowing that it would not misdirect me. I ran as fast as could go. As I got up to the rock, my staff thrust itself to the base of the rock, catapulting me up and over the rock all the way to entrance of the cave where I was able to enter to safety.

I could not say the same about all the Hubearians. As quickly as the giant birds had appeared, they were gone. But left behind were lots of large rocks and several dead Hubearians. In fact, there were seventeen dead Hubearians. We spent the rest of the day gathering the dead bodies and placing them in their tombs. As the sun set, we gathered around a large fire and had a ceremony giving the Creator thanks for each fallen Hubearian.

Valcor told me, "Such is way of life for us right now. It's good versus evil. It seems evil is gaining strength. I truly don't know how much longer we can resist evil's advancements. The only thing I do know is that we must somehow win." I replayed those words over and over in my head as I lay down to sleep. I felt so much pressure on Chelsea and me. Many lives, in fact, an entire land depended on us doing what we were brought here to do. I just didn't know how we were going to do it. I looked at Chelsea and thought about all this. She was sound asleep. But for me, it would be a long time before I could soundly sleep again.

The Swamp

The new day brought with it a new challenge. As part of our training, Chelsea and I had to take a trip escorted by Valcor and his best warriors. We were going to have to probe the entire land east of the Crystal Sea known as the living forest and some areas west of the Crystal Sea, which we knew were under the control of evil influences.

With the cave as our base we left from there. There were twenty-five Hubearians that accompanied Chelsea and me. The only weapons we carried were our staffs and each of us had our own backpack of supplies. After a couple of hours of walking through the forest we came across a swampy area. Soon, the land which we were walking on left us, We found ourselves walking in about a foot of water. The stench was unbearable. I asked Valcor, who was leading the trip, what was the source of the horrid smell. He turned slowly, raised his hand, and softly said, "What you smell is the presence of creatures that live in this dirty water. Now be quiet because they don't see well but can hear extremely well."

At that point neither Chelsea nor I knew what to expect next. The water was moving all around us and I could tell the Hubearians' alert level had spiked. They were constantly looking at the water around their legs as if something was swimming under the water's surface.

Then unexpectedly a Hubearian just a few yards behind me disappeared underneath the water. Everyone stopped and looked like statues frozen in place. Our staffs were raised above our heads in a striking position. I still did not know what we could be striking at but I had a feeling it wasn't anything nice.

At the back of our line another Hubearian was sucked under the surface. This time the water was stirred aggressively as whatever had pulled the Hubearian down was using a lot of force. Then just like that the staff of the Hubearian was spit out of the water in two pieces. Whatever was below us had enough strength to snap our staffs. The prospects of what creature this may be was very disturbing to Chelsea and me as we looked at each other with a fearful anticipation of what was going to happen next.

Everything got quiet and the waters became still. It was almost spooky how calm things had suddenly become. It was like the calm before the storm. At that moment, from underneath the water rose hideous creatures. I didn't have time to count them but it seemed like a dozen or so. They were around eight feet tall and covered in scales. Each creature had short arms but from what I could tell no legs. They were empowered by their extremely long and thick tails. Their heads had long snouts that opened wide enough to swallow a creature my size. Their snouts contained countless teeth that looked like they were used to shred flesh from the bone.

"Be prepared to engage these creatures!" Valcor shouted to Chelsea and me. "They are sneaky creatures who like to attack from below where you can't see them. Allow your staff to watch their movements and if they come at you, strike for the end of their snouts or eyes. Those are their weak spots. Whatever you do don't let them look into your eyes because they will attempt to hypnotize you and then gobble you up."

At that point each of the creatures moved towards all of us by diving under the water. All I could think about was not looking in their eyes but watching around my legs and feet. One thing that really scared me was the prospects of being grabbed without knowing where it was coming from.

Water began to swirl all around me and I noticed the water was swirling around every one of us. It seemed like a diversionary tactic so that we could not tell where their attacks were coming from. At that point my staff warned me to look behind me. I turned and saw a flash in the water coming right at me. I quickly thrust my staff towards the creature striking it and causing it to retreat.

Now all of us were engaged in battle with these creatures. Loud roars consumed the air around me as the creatures were attempting to consume as many of us as possible. Valcor gave a loud shout of instruction to all of us when he said, "Move to the other side of the swamp as quick as you can. They only live in the water and cannot survive on land."

So we began moving towards the land on the other side of the swamp. Chelsea and I ran side by side to protect one another against these creatures. From what seemed like nowhere, one of the creatures leaped from the water towards me. I thought I was a goner for sure because I didn't have time to react. But Chelsea happened to be looking in that direction when the creature leaped. She was able to use her staff to strike the creature a precise hit on the tip of its snout. Immediately the creature fell to the water and swam off. "Thank you, Chelsea," I told her, "it's a good thing you were watching out for me."

As we were fighting and running it seemed the creatures knew we were attempting to get to dry land because their efforts to catch us grew more intense as if they knew their time was running out. As I looked ahead of me I noticed Valcor was engaged in a fierce battle with two of the creatures. There was a creature on each side of Valcor snapping their snouts. He was doing his best to fight off the creatures but they were so big and powerful he was losing the fight. So Chelsea and I caught up with Valcor and each of us joined the fight. Chelsea took one of the creatures and I took the other. The tide had turned on the creatures. They now were outnumbered as the three of us fought the two of them.

Chelsea had become quite good with her staff. She was striking blows to the head and body of the creature she was fighting. At one point I noticed she had knocked out several teeth from the creature's snout. Then with one quick blow hit both of the creature's eyes sending the creature on retreat.

Chelsea then joined with me in fighting my creature. Valcor moved to the back side of the creature and we had the creature surrounded. I guess the creature realized there would be easier meals because at that point it just went under water and was gone.

"Let's keep moving!" I yelled. So we moved closer to the edge of the land. As I reached land I excitedly spoke to Chelsea, "We made it, girlfriend!" I noticed Chelsea didn't answer. I turned to look at her and noticed she was not by my side like before. Wondering where she was I turned to survey the swamp and I saw her still in the water. "Chelsea," I screamed in horror. "Don't look, Chelsea!" But my words were too late. She had somehow looked into the eyes of one of the creatures and become frozen. The creature was getting in position to snatch her and take her under the water.

I yelled to her, "I'm coming, Chelsea—hang on!" Valcor tried to tell me to stay on the land and let the other Hubearians in the water help her but I was not about to stand around and see my best friend from my land get eaten by some ugly beast. So without regards for myself I leaped back into the water and made my way to Chelsea.

Just as the creature was making its move to take Chelsea under, I lunged in between the creature and Chelsea, startling the creature. It looked at me intently, trying to get me to look in its eyes. I knew better and looked at its body underneath its snout.

I began swinging feverishly at the beast to get it away from Chelsea. As I swung for the tip of its snout, it moved out of the way and grabbed my staff with its snout, gripping my staff with its teeth. I heard my staff make a noise of pain. I stood there with both my hands on my staff while the creature gripped my staff in its snout. The creature was applying more pressure and my staff made more noises of agony. I knew that any time the creature could snap my staff, killing my new friend and leaving me defenseless to protect Chelsea or myself.

My staff began speaking to me as it felt the pressure of the creature's snout splinter its wooden frame. My staff told me, "I will protect you as long as I can. Let me go. While the creature is chewing me you will have time to get Chelsea and yourself to land." What a brave act. My staff was willing to give its life in order to save mine. For some reason the first thought in mind was the old saying my parents taught me growing up. They used to say, "You will know a true friend if they are willing to lay down their life to save yours. Sacrifice is the sign of true love."

At that moment I had to make a decision. Logic told me to leave my staff, take Chelsea, and run. But my heart told me I could not leave my staff behind. So I listened to my heart and spoke back to my staff, "You have proven your devotion to me and now I will prove mine to you. I will not leave you or Chelsea. The Creator will rescue us."

Out of the corner of my eye I caught the figure of something floating beside me. I looked down and saw half the broken staff from one of the fallen Hubearians. I kicked water in the face of Chelsea and she woke from her trance. I told her to pick up the broken staff and toss it in air. As she did this, I let go of my staff with my right hand and caught the broken staff with my hand and in the same motion thrust the broken edge of the staff into the side of the creature. The creature instantly let go of my staff and screeched in pain. As blood from the creature began spilling out in the water, I held on to my staff in my left hand and grabbed Chelsea with my right hand and we all headed for land.

We, along with the rest of the Hubearians, were able to make it to land safely. We all looked back to the water and watched the creatures converge on the wounded creature, tearing it apart in a gruesome act of cannibalism. They didn't care the creature was one of their own; they just sensed a wounded animal and put it out of its misery.

As we lay on the dry land catching our breath, Chelsea looked at me and thanked me for coming to her rescue. I simply told her that is what friends are for. Then I thanked my staff for its willingness to give its life for me. My staff replied, "Friends sacrifice for friends. Besides, you are not only my friend but the one who will make things right again."

After a short time of rest and recuperation, we gathered ourselves and began to move on. Through all that had happened we did lose two Hubearians in the fight. I felt sad for their families but their sacrifice just motivated me to keep focused on my calling. I did not want their deaths to be in vain.

The Trees

We had been walking for quite a while when we came upon a hillside overlooking a valley filled with trees. As we looked at the valley I began to get a feeling of my home. There was a tremendous sense of peace that came across me.

The trees looked just like the old shade tree from the park in which Chelsea and I had been playing in before we met the unicorn. In this valley I saw shade trees of all sizes and shapes. I turned to Chelsea and asked, "Don't those trees remind of our shade tree back home?"

Chelsea responded, "Yeah, I want to go home."

Valcor said to us, "You are looking at the valley of dreams. All the trees you see in this valley are very much alive and have a special ability. They have the ability to allow you to experience your dreams."

I asked skeptically, "What? How does a tree allow you to live out your dreams? That doesn't make any sense."

Reacting to my doubt, Valcor continued, "How can you ask such questions and have such doubt? After what you have seen so far you should expect anything. These trees are very kind and gentle. They love to serve other creatures. Their way of serving is to give us our dreams. They feel it makes us happy."

Chelsea asked, "What kind of dreams?"

Valcor said, "Any dream you have. This valley is the most popular place this side of the Crystal Sea. All creatures, great and small, come here to find rest from their struggles."

I mentioned that the trees in the valley reminded me of the shade tree back at my home. Valcor then gave a fascinating response. He told Chelsea and me that the shade tree in our park was from this valley. It had been planted there by the unicorn after my great grandfather had returned from the land of the Crystal Sea. The purpose of the shade tree was to help watch for the chosen one. Valcor went on to tell us that once I had been identified as the chosen one, the tree's sole mission had switched to bringing me a peace of mind and allowing me to live my dreams in hopes of bringing me here to fulfill my mission.

"You mean to tell me that old shade tree has been spying on me my whole life?" I asked.

Valcor said, "Yes. It has been communicating to us your whole life giving us progress reports on you until you were ready to come help us. I'm sure you have enjoyed the tree."

I said, "True. When I first noticed the tree, it seemed magical. That shade tree is truly a great tree."

Valcor then looked at all of us standing on the hill and said, "Why don't we take a short break from our trip and go live one of our dreams." Everyone around us shouted with excitement and ran to the valley. Valcor, Chelsea, and I stood there as we watched all the Hubearians rush to the trees, each one finding a spot at the base of a tree and resting against the tree. It seemed therapeutic for the Hubearians.

Then I noticed something about the trees I wasn't expecting. After a Hubearian rested against the trunk of one of the shade trees, the tree would move in a manner that made it look like it truly cared for the creature resting at its trunk. It reminded me of a mother hen caring for its chicks. The trees almost seemed like they were snuggling the Hubearians as they rested.

Valcor asked, "Do you want to give it a try?" Chelsea and I looked at each other. I'm sure there was a look of hesitancy on our faces as we agreed to go down in the valley and find a tree.

My staff at that point began to speak, "Don't be afraid. The shade trees love you and will bring you happiness."

So with the encouragement of my trusting staff we all three entered the valley of dreams. Valcor found a tree, leaving Chelsea and me to find one on our own. We cautiously walked around the valley, checking out different trees. Finally, Chelsea and I found two trees side by side and we both lay against the trunks of our trees.

It didn't take long for me to feel comfortable enough to relax and close my eyes. Suddenly I found myself dreaming. What a wonderful dream it was. I was home playing with dog in my backyard. My dog was a great friend to me. I could see my dad cooking on the grill my favorite food, cheeseburgers. My mom was resting on our hammock getting some sun. I found myself missing all the simple things in life I had taken for granted.

For a long time I had thought my family life was a curse. But now, after being away and having this dream, the shade tree was helping me see just how great of a life I had with my family.

I had a couple of other dreams as I laid there at the base of that old shade tree. The tree was making me happy. I felt such peace. I could have laid there forever. But just as easy as it was to relax and begin dreaming, suddenly I felt the tree was telling me it was time to wake up. I slowly began opening my eyes because I was very drowsy. As my eyes came into focus I saw Chelsea, Valcor, and all the Hubearians standing in front of me with big grins on their faces. "What?" I asked. They just laughed at me. Then I realized why. I had been dreaming so well that I had drooled all over myself. I quickly wiped the drool away and hopped up, hoping to show my toughness.

Valcor said, "Don't worry about slobbering on yourself. It happens to the best of us."

Chelsea said, "Yeah, you should have seen me. I looked like I had been dunking for apples." I laughed as I thought about that.

Before we left the valley I turned and looked up at the shade tree I had been resting under. It made the same sounds as the one in my park. The tree was so inviting and relaxing. I felt very loved and very safe while under its care. I thanked the tree for its time, turned to Valcor and wondered if it was time to move on. Valcor began leading us out of the valley and as we left I thought of how better my land would be if each person could take time to rest under an old shade tree.

The Ambush

As we continued on our journey to the Crystal Sea, Valcor began explaining to us what we faced on the other side. "The other side of the Sea contains many creatures that are evil, desiring to free the beast and gain control of the entire land of the Crystal Sea. Right now they are lacking leadership because the beast is still frozen. If we can reach the beast and destroy him then the evil present in our land will disappear. However, if the beast is freed, then I'm afraid the beast will be more determined than ever to conquer our land.

"I'm sure the evil armies that lie on the other side of the sea are aware of your arrival, Abigail. They know the prophecy well enough to sense urgency in freeing the beast and stopping you. As we get closer to the Crystal Sea we ultimately get closer to the enemy. This means their attacks on us will most likely increase. Be ready."

We finally reached a spot where Valcor thought we could rest for the night, so we set up camp. Later that night we were all sleeping comfortably in our shelters. For some reason I was restless. It might have been because of the day's events or maybe because of the fears of what still lay ahead of me. Whatever the reason, I couldn't sleep. So I decided to get up and stretch my legs.

As I walked around our camp I noticed a silence coming from the woods around us. It was so quiet that I got goose bumps on my arms. Something just did not seem right to me. But I decided it was just me being paranoid because everyone else was sound asleep. So I walked outside our camp and gazed at the bright lights in the sky thinking about everything that I was going through.

As I was thinking about everything, I heard some noises coming from a nearby hedge of brush. It was soft noise like a noise a small animal would make so I didn't really pay it any attention. Then out of the corner of my eye I noticed some movement from that same area. I turned to look and as I did something a lot bigger than a small animal came out of the thick brush behind me.

I gulped and turned around. There in front of me was a creature that stood six feet tall. It was covered in a matted fur and smelled to the point of me wanting to vomit. The creature had claws like that of a sloth and fangs like that of a saber tooth tiger.

As I stood in fear of this creature I heard another noise behind me. So I slowly looked behind me. There was another creature behind me, gazing at me as if it wanted to do me harm. This creature was different from the first. This creature stood even taller. It didn't have any fur but was wrapped in a primitive cloth that covered its midsection and part of its upper body. In one hand it carried a big club and in the other hand it carried some kind of weapon with a blade attached. This creature was ugly. Its skin was hairless and wrinkled. It had three eyes across its forehead and a mouth with teeth hanging out.

While looking at this creature I noticed movement to my right and left. I quickly looked in both directions and saw yet two more creatures. Both were hideous looking and each had weapons in both of their hands. At this point I felt like I was a goner. All four creatures were looking at me with intent to bring me harm. Then they started moving slowly towards me. I realized I had left my staff in my shelter so I did not have any means to defend myself. Then doubt began to fill my mind. I started focusing on my age, my gender, and anything else that could discourage me from getting away from these creatures.

As the creatures moved in on me, the bushes around us began moving. Then they jumped out of the ground and ran towards us. This startled the creatures. Hundreds of bushes, shrubs, and other plants gathered around the creatures and me, forming a barrier between the creatures and me. This was confusing the creatures to the point of the creatures ignoring me and trying to get the plants off of and away from them.

As the creatures were preoccupied with the onslaught of plant life I remembered what Chelsea's staff said when they first met. The staff made a comment about bushes being able to run. Apparently these bushes were trying to protect me from the creatures. So I seized the moment. The bushes opened a path for me to escape and I took it. I was able to make it back to camp. At that point I woke everyone up and began warning of the impending danger.

Just as I finished, a large number of creatures came rushing at us from the surrounding brush. We were completely caught off guard. Valcor yelled, "Ambush! Grab your staffs and protect the humans!" Each Hubearian made a mad dash for their staffs. Some were intercepted by creatures before they could make it to their staffs. It was complete chaos. Chelsea and I were in the center of camp as we watched a battle happening right before our eyes.

Valcor screamed at us, "Here are your staffs!" He threw us our staffs and both Chelsea and I caught them. Instantly we were engaged in battle with creatures that looked so hideous I wanted to hide my face from them. I found myself in conflict with a short but very determined creature. Its appearance reminded me of images I had of what a demon might look like. It was grey and black with sores all over its body. The creature was about half my height but stronger than I would ever be. It fought me with a ferociousness that penetrated my very soul.

It took everything I had to keep from getting clobbered by this creature. Its ability to handle a staff was just as good if not better than my own. During our fight the creature connected with a swing that hit my left ankle, bringing me to one knee. Then the creature lunged for me. I used my staff to hold the creature off me but the creature's strength was too strong. I was pushed all the way to the ground on my back. I was doing everything I could do to keep the creature off of me.

As it pressed against my staff I could feel it getting closer. Then the creature got so close that its ugly face was just inches above my face. It stared at me with a smirk across its face. Its spittle and drool began to drip on my face. Then the creature spoke. It said, "So you are the chosen one. Do you really think you can accomplish your mission, you puny human? You are but a little human girl. What can you do? I have killed bigger creatures for dinner. In fact, once I kill you I will have you for dinner and your head as a trophy."

As it was talking, blood and small insect looking creatures were all in its mouth and sharp teeth. I tried as hard as I could to push the creature away from my face but it was too strong. The creature pressed closer and closer to me. The creature began laughing as it pulled out a long stone blade from its garment. It raised the blade above its head ready to drive the blade deep in my body when out of the blue came help. Someone had used their staff and knocked the creature off of me, allowing me to get back on my feet.

It was Chelsea. Chelsea had just freed herself from fighting a creature of her own and saw I needed help so she rushed to my aid. "Thank God for you, Chelsea. I thought that creature was going to put an end to me," I said to her.

She replied, "Not if I can help it!" I knew I had a good friend in Chelsea. She was like a guardian for me. I was thankful I could count on a friend like her. Then we both went after the creature who had pinned me to the ground. The creature was strong but not strong enough to handle both of us. So the creature withdrew to the brush out of fear.

The battle around us was still raging. I noticed a few Hubearians lying on the ground, either hurt or dead. But I noticed many more evil creatures on the ground, dead from the battle. The battle went on for hours. We were severely outnumbered by the creatures. As the battle wore on, the Hubearians began forming a circle around Chelsea and me. Slowly the circle got tighter and tighter until there was not any more room for us to move.

When this happened, the creatures stopped fighting and looked at us as if to say, "We have you now." The Hubearians held strong and were willing to continue the fight but did look confused as to why the evil creatures had stopped fighting just when they had us pinned in a tight circle with nowhere to go.

The evil creatures opened their circle of advance just enough to allow one of their own to approach us. I noticed a shadowy figure walking towards us and stopping in front of Valcor, who was in front of us. This creature looked like a mix of several different things. It had the head of a reptile, the body of an ox, and the wings of a black unicorn. I looked at this creature intently and could tell it was well respected by all the other evil creatures around us.

Valcor spoke to the creature, "So Rapator, you are behind this ambush."

The creature replied, "Did you expect anyone else? Who else could put together such an ambush as this? I will have to say I am impressed you have lasted this long. Most creatures would have either given up or been killed a long time ago."

Valcor responded, "You know me well enough to know I will never give up, especially to you. What is it you want from me?"

Rapator mocked, "From you! Valcor, you will never understand me. Why I want nothing from you. This ambush has nothing to do with you. You are just a mere hurdle to what I want. I want the humans. Word is it that you have the chosen one in your presence. I aim to relieve you of that burden."

Valcor fired back, "The humans are not a burden. The prophecy speaks of the chosen one…"

Rapator interrupted, "The prophecy! You mean the myth! Our land's myth speaks of one who will come along and restore our land to its original goodness. Blah blah blah. You don't really believe that nonsense do you? Come on! How can a little human girl such as the ones you are protecting do what your so called prophecy suggests?"

Valcor responded, "If you don't believe in the prophecy then why are you here attempting to harm these humans?"

Rapator said, "Because I enjoy inflicting fear in this great land of ours. Now, I am going to give you a choice. You can either hand over the humans and I can let you return to your cave, without being harmed. Or, we can finish this battle by killing you, the rest of Hubearians, and the humans. What shall it be?"

There was silence for a moment on behalf of Valcor which made me nervous. Then Valcor answered, "I guess you are right. The prophecy could very well be a myth which would make my defense of these humans pointless.

Why should I jeopardize the lives of my fellow Hubearians over these two outsiders? Go ahead and take them."

I voiced my opinion on the matter, "What! Now wait just a minute. What are you doing, Valcor? You can't be serious about this?"

Valcor said, "I'm afraid so. You are not worth dying for."

Rapator chimed in, "Good choice, my brother. I'm glad you decided to make a sensible choice. You see, girls, I am Valcor's brother. Can't you see the resemblance? Way back when the first two humans came along I decided to follow the one who wanted to rule this land. Over time my appearance changed. I used to look like Valcor but now I am much improved."

Chelsea asked Valcor, "I thought you said the changing of appearance was just a human thing?"

Valcor replied, "I was wrong."

Chelsea went on to say, "I guess we were wrong in trusting you as well. We thought you were one of the good guys."

Valcor said, "Sorry to disappoint you," with disgust in his voice.

With everyone fixed on our conversation, Tabukoo came running out from behind some rocks. But it wasn't just Tabukoo. Behind Tabukoo were a countless number of creatures just like Tabukoo. They all rushed the evil creatures and engaging them in a massive struggle of control. I was overcome with emotion as I witnessed Tabukoo and his fellow creatures overcome the evil ones who had us pressed in a tight circle.

Valcor and the rest of the Hubearians joined in the confrontation. This time we had the surprise and the battle was ours to win. I watched Rapator flee by flying upwards and out of sight, leaving his evil hoard of creatures to suffer defeat. One by one the evil creatures were either killed or they fled the scene until finally the battle had come to an end.

After it was all over I fell down in exhaustion only to be comforted by Valcor and Tabukoo. As I looked in the face of Valcor I said, "You had Chelsea and me fooled there for a moment."

He replied, "Please forgive me, chosen one, but I had to allow my brother to think I was serious about giving you up in order to gain the element of surprise. Know that I would never betray your friendship." Those words were good enough for me to understand what had just happened.

I regained my strength and we all attempted to get a little rest as the new day dawned over the mountaintops. In my sleep I dreamed about the turmoil that poor Valcor had to be experiencing because of the division between himself and his brother. Knowing now about that division motivated me even more to restore things to what they used to be.

The Skies

The new day brought with it a new feeling of safety because Tabukoo and his fellow creatures were with us. The new day also brought with it a couple of new commands from Valcor. Valcor told us that since we had just experienced a long and hard fight the night before that we would only travel a short distance today. This command turned out to be a smart one as all of us were very tired. If there was one thing I had already learned was that getting enough rest was essential to survival in this land.

After learning that we had a short day of travel ahead of us, Valcor filled us in on where we were headed. We were told that our goal over the next few days was to make it to the Crystal Sea and that site would be the point when we would head back to the cave.

When I heard about us heading for the Crystal Sea, I became very nervous, yet excited at the same time. I knew of the history of this land's struggle of good versus evil and how my great grandfather held back evil at the Crystal Sea by defeating the beast. Now, it appeared, I was going to get a chance to witness where that epic battle took place.

We packed up our supplies and began heading towards our next destination. Soon after we got started I asked Valcor if we had any stops before we reached the Crystal Sea. Valcor told me to just be ready for anything. His only plan was to make two more camps before we reached the sea, but after all we had already encountered I knew a lot could happen along the way.

We had only been traveling for about an hour when I took a survey of our group. Many had lost their lives on this trip. Another lesson I was learning was that life is such a fragile gift. At any moment it could be taken away. I longed to hold my mom just one more time. Often my mom and I would fight over what now seemed like petty things. If I could just speak to her again I would tell her how much I love her and how thankful I was for her direction and devotion. Thinking of my mom gave me the courage to move forward and the motivation to not let anything bad happen to me.

Just as I made that promise to myself, I was suddenly pushed to ground. As soon as I hit the ground I heard what sounded like a miniature explosion off to my side. While still face first in the dirt I could hear the Hubearians warning of attacks from the skies. While on the dirt I rolled over and looked upwards. What my eyes beheld was that of a flying creature so terrifying that even Tabukoo seemed to flee from its presence.

These flying creatures were not anything close to being a type of bird. They seemed to have a reptilian look to them but it was difficult for me to get a good look at them. Things were happening all around me and the flying creatures were moving so fast and so high that I could not get a good look at them.

One thing I could see was that they were big and mean. Tabukoo, Valcor, and all the other Hubearians were taking cover…and for good reason. These flying creatures could shoot fire out their eyes. Apparently one attempted to cook me before a Hubearian pushed me out the way earlier. Shooting fire out of their eyes was not the only thing they could do. Their wings could somehow distribute a gray powder substance that eats through whatever it touched. It reminded me of acid.

So these flying creatures were shooting at us with fire and dropping an acid powder that brought pain and destruction on any living thing it touched. No wonder every creature around me was running for shelter. Tabukoo and his friends were heaving up rocks at the flying creatures trying to protect all of us. I happened to glance over at one of Tabukoo's friends as he swung his arm back preparing to throw a large rock. Just at that moment fire reigned from the sky striking him in the back and setting him ablaze. He was burnt to a crisp in a matter of seconds.

Hubearians were running all around me while screaming in pain from the acidic powder of the flying creatures. That powder was even more dangerous than the flames because it was light enough that could be blown anywhere. So many of us could be out of sight yet still come in contact with the powder and be thrust into sharp pain.

My thoughts quickly turned to Chelsea. As I looked around me I could not see her anywhere. I began moving from rock to rock and bush to bush trying to locate her. It was complete chaos around me. Creatures were screaming in pain on the ground and creatures screaming in triumph in the air. I knew it would be very difficult to find her but I had to try. She was my best friend. I secured myself behind a large tree trunk and began surveying the area in an attempt to find Chelsea. As I was looking with one eye on the sky and one eye on the ground I heard a rushing sound coming for my head. I knew it was the sound of flames coming towards me so I ducked down as quickly as I could just under the rushing flames that a flying creature had sent towards me. While ducked under cover I was looking up and I saw grey specks falling towards me from above me. I thought they were ashes from the singed wood above my head so I didn't move. Then a few of those specks landed on my left arm. Pain rushed through my arm and throughout my entire body like I had never felt before. I had been hit by the powdery acid dropped from above. I quickly moved out of the way of the remaining specks that were falling but I could escape the horrifying pain that I was already experiencing.

Tears filled my eyes and slid down my face. It felt like my left arm was on fire. My skin was developing holes up and down my arm where the specks had made contact. I tore off a piece of my sleeve and rapped it around the holes on my arm. Then I struggled to my feet to continue to look for Chelsea.

I was having such a hard time seeing because of the smoke and debris. Everything seemed like a blur. Then I heard Chelsea's voice off to my right. She was screaming, "Get away from me. Get away from me."

I recognized terror in her voice. At that point I began yelling to Chelsea to tell me where she was so I could help her. She then began yelling back to me, "Help me, Abigail! Please help me!" Over and over she screamed for my help. But I felt useless as I could not seem to find her. My only hope was to lock on to her voice and locate her with my hearing.

As I moved slowly to my right I could sense I was getting closer. I could hear Chelsea screaming for help and struggling to hold something off of her. Then I heard Chelsea scream, "Abigail! Help me! No!" Chelsea's scream sent chills all over my body as I picked up my pace to find her. I was just praying she was okay.

I finally made my way to a small clearing in the smoke. There among the crackling sounds of fire in the brush and the smoke that accompanied the flames, I saw Chelsea's staff lying on the ground. It was charred from the heat of the flames. Chelsea, however, was nowhere to be found. Her staff began weakly coughing to get my attention. I kneeled down as the staff began to speak. "Chelsea and I were engaged with two of those flying creatures. I tried to help her. I did my best to block the flames from her eyes, the claws from her feet, but they were too strong for me."

At that moment Valcor, Tabukoo, and the others encircled us. The staff went on to say, "They took her! They took her! I'm sorry I couldn't stop them. You've got to rescue her." At that moment the staff closed its eyes and broke in half. The flames it had so bravely fought off to save Chelsea had taken the life of the staff.

Valcor placed his hand on my shoulder and told me that the flying creatures were gone. After hearing what Chelsea's staff had told me, Valcor concluded that the flying creatures were sent to capture Chelsea and me. He went on to say that the flying creatures must have become satisfied with just Chelsea but warned they could return for me at any moment.

I was in shock. My best friend had been taken captive by a band of evil creatures and she was on her own. My best friend was gone. At this point I did not even know if she was still alive. All I could think about was her terrifying screams for help and me not being able to help her. She must have been scared out of her mind and it was my fault. She came to this land with me because she just happened to be with me when the unicorn showed up. Now she might not even be alive. I was definitely at the lowest point of my life.

Tabukoo spoke gently to encourage me that we needed to press on. If we were going to have a chance to save Chelsea we needed to get out of the area we were in. So everyone around me began gathering themselves and what belongings survived the attack. As they all did what they needed to do, I remained at the sight of Chelsea's fallen staff. I reflected on some of my best memories of Chelsea. She had been such a great friend over the years. And now, I stared upon her staff who had given its life to save her life.

My staff tried to comfort me when it said to me, "Abigail. I told you that I would give everything I have to protect you. That's what Chelsea's staff did for her. You must understand that if her staff was still alive when we arrived at the scene that means that Chelsea is still alive. Her staff would not have remained alive if Chelsea wasn't. Now rise up. You are Chelsea's only hope. Abigail, you are the only hope that any of us have who desire for good to win this land back. I will stay by your side every step of the way to gain the freedom of your friend."

Listening to my staff did comfort me that it wasn't too late to help Chelsea. Although she had experienced horrible terror and been captured by evil creatures and taken to an evil place on her own, we still had a chance to make a difference for her and this land. So I rose up. I thought for a moment of my earlier thoughts about the fragileness of life. I remembered all the times my mother told me how she believed in me, and then…turned to Valcor and said, "Let's go get her and win back your land, to the glory of the Creator!"

The Enemy

We continued to march on. The whole time we were walking I was still waging a battle. Not a battle around me, but a battle within me. My mind was harboring two lines of thought. One line of thought was telling me that I was way over my head and that I needed to stop while I still had my life, and go home. The other line of thought was telling me to press on because my best friend and an entire land depended on me. My natural desire was to listen to the first line of thought and run for my life. After all, I was only thirteen. How much could I possibly do? However, my love for Chelsea and my desire to do what is right gave me the strength to overcome my cowardliness and press on.

As we continued on our journey to the Crystal Sea, Valcor heard a noise coming from the hilltop to our left. It sounded like some type of animal running through the leaves on the ground. I could tell that whatever it was, was coming closer to us because the noise became louder and louder. Valcor positioned his staff, ready to take on whatever it was coming at us. Then out of the bushes came forth this small furry animal. The animal was very odd looking. Its body was the size and shape of a common rat. However, it had a tail like that of a bird, yet furry, and feet the size of a large, hairy dog.

When Valcor spotted the animal he quickly lowered his staff and breathed a sigh of relief. This animal apparently was friendly animal and not one out to bring us harm. Valcor said, "Roto, you scared me. Next time give me some kind of warning before you approach us like that."

Roto replied, "SSSSSooorrrrryy." Little Roto stuttered his speech. Roto went on to say, "Mr. Valcor. I just returned from the enemy's camp on the west side of the Crystal Sea and I have a report."

Valcor explained to all of us that Roto was an excellent spy for us and had been sent to examine the enemy's camp and to try to figure out their plans for stopping us from destroying the beast. Then Valcor motioned for Roto to continue. "The enemy is large in number. Many creatures from all over our land have joined forces with the beast's army. I think that a lot of them have done so out of fear instead of desire. Rapator has threatened many of the creatures of the land with execution if they don't follow him."

I interrupted Roto to ask if he had seen Chelsea. Roto went on to say, "I did see a human creature like you...a girl."

I responded, "Yes, that's Chelsea! Is she okay? Are they hurting her?" Roto responded, "At this point she has not been harmed. But Rapator plans to use her as leverage to free the beast. I heard Rapator and some of his evil leaders making plans to exchange the girl for the beast. They went on to say that if you harmed the beast they would kill the girl. Also, they plan on killing the human if you don't free the beast."

Valcor then asked, "What creatures make up Rapator's army?" Roto listed some creatures I did not know about.

Roto said, "I saw the Bullerios, the Lazniks, the Sniklestaints, the Delfins, the Mezerians, and the Grazzilonies. These make up what I call the evil six...six groups that are teaming with your brother, Rapator, to free the beast and take over all our land. I also saw many individual creatures who have defected from their homes to join Rapator, including a few Hubearians."

Valcor took a few seconds to ponder what Roto had told him. For the first time since I had known Valcor he seemed to worry. Then Valcor softly said, "Hubearians in the enemy's camp. That makes me sad. How could any creature, especially one of my own, think that what the enemy stands for is a just cause? It sounds like my brother has been successful in assembling a good number of the creature groups of our land. He has gathered six of the creature groups. There are only twenty-one known creature groups in our land. We have eight of those groups. His six and our eight equals fourteen. That means there are still seven groups that are neutral at this point. I think that what we need to do is visit those seven groups and find out where they stand. Thank you, Roto, for your report. You may return and be careful. I want another report soon." Roto lowered his head and ran off back into the woods in which he came from.

After Roto's departure I looked at Valcor and asked him about the creatures that Roto had mentioned, "Who are the creatures that Roto mentioned? You know, the Bullerios, the Delfins, and the others?"

Valcor briefly explained each group. "The Grazzilonies are a large number of creatures that live on the west side of the sea. They stand three feet tall and are very thin. Because of their size they are very fast. In fact, in battle it is almost impossible to defeat them because they can move faster than anyone else. They use grass canvas to cover their hairless bodies, making them very hard to see in the wilderness.

"The Sniklestaints are just the opposite. They are somewhere between ten and eighteen feet tall. They don't move fast like the Grazzilonies but make up for their lack of speed in their strength. One Sniklestaint is as strong as ten Tabukoo's. They have only one eye in the front of their head and one eye on the back side of their head making it very difficult to sneak up on them. The only weapons they use are whatever they can find. They'll use rocks, logs, or whatever is lying around to fight against you.

"I am surprised to hear about the Delfins being part of the enemy group. They must be there out of fear like Roto spoke of. The Delfins are normally a peaceful group of creatures. They can live in water as well as on land. They are called Delfins because they have fins that are not only used for swimming in the water but also are strong enough to be used for legs when walking on water. They can command water to move from one location to another. They have some very sharp teeth in their snouts and are about seven feet in length.

"The Lazniks are a very curious bunch of creatures. From the reports we received from the unicorn when he was making his trips to your land, he would describe a creature there that was similar in appearance. I think you call it a squirrel. Lazniks can live in the trees and travel from tree to tree quicker than a lot of us can run on the ground. They look like your squirrel but are much bigger. I would say as big as you.

"The Mezerians are a difficult group to say the least. Ever since your great grandfather's presence in our land, they have been very bitter and resentful towards any of us who harbored your great grandfather. I guess it should be no surprise that they chose to follow the beast. The Mezerians would have no problem gutting you like a ripe melon if given the opportunity. Be careful around one of them. You will know a Mezerians by the red in their eyes. When you look into their eyes, you can see red located in the inside corner of each eye. That is the only way to tell them apart from other creatures sometimes because they can take on the form of any creature. And they will do so in order to gain the advantage when in battle.

"Finally, Roto mentioned the Bullerios. A Bullerio is a creature that is all muscle. To touch one is like touching a solid rock. They have black snouts that they blow out their hot breath when they are ready to attack you. If one comes running after you, don't try to stand your ground because you will get trampled on. They only way to win against an attacking Bullerio is distract him long enough to get a hard hit across his snout. The best way to distract a Bullerio is flash the color red. They hate that color more than anything. If a Bullerio sees the color red he will forget everything else and attempt to destroy whatever it is that is red."

After hearing about all the creatures that stood in my way of accomplishing my purpose, the thought of failure came back. How in the world could I, Abigail Parker, a thirteen-year-old girl from Florida, overcome all that stood in my way of accomplishing my purpose? Why I could not even make the basketball team back in my school. I have a cousin who is a better artist than I am. Even Chelsea's little brother is faster than me when we race. There is no way I can do what is expected of me.

My staff began to speak to me at that moment, "Abigail. I see doubt all over your face. Listen closely. Remember the prophecy. Remember all that has been told to you and taught to you. Remember what you have done so far. Maybe most importantly, remember that the Creator, who put all of us in motion, has chosen you to fulfill this purpose. You can do this."

Out of fear, I spoke back to my staff, "Maybe the Creator doesn't know what he's doing. How can a thirteen-year-old girl like me make a difference? I am not good at much of anything. I'm not the fastest runner. I'm not the strongest human. I don't have any special abilities. How can someone so average make such a big difference? I think the Creator made a mistake if He chose me to fulfill the prophecy. I can think of so many other humans better qualified."

Tabukoo heard our conversation and replied to me, "Abigail. All those things that you mentioned may be true. You might not be the strongest, fastest, or as special as you think others are, but that is exactly why the Creator has chosen you. Don't you get it? You are perfect for the job. The Creator wants all of us in this land he has created to return to a perfect relationship with him. The only way that can happen is if the beast is destroyed and evil is defeated. Good must win. In your weakness the Creator will triumph and we will live in a good land once more."

After listening to Tabukoo I could sort of understand what he was trying to say. It all seemed so overwhelming to me however. My mind hurt from the thinking about it all. I guess it was just a matter of accepting my role in all of it. Maybe that is what my mom meant when she would tell me she believed in me. My mom would tell me that believing is not always a result from seeing. Strong faith had to come from what we could not see. Anybody could believe with their eyes, but it took an extraordinary person to believe with their heart.

Perhaps my strongest enemy at this point in all that was happening was not Rapator or the beast or the evil army that wanted to kill me. Perhaps my strongest enemy at this point was, in fact, me. The struggle within me to accept and believe in myself as the right person for this purpose was real and sometimes too strong to handle. If I could come to grips with myself within the boundaries of what I was called to do, then maybe things would not be as hard as they currently were. I remembered how my mother spoke about a peace that comes with faith. As of right now, I was experiencing a conflict, not peace. Before the conflict in this land could be settled, I was going to have to settle the conflict within me.

The Maltoids

After a good night's rest we set out the next morning hoping to reach the Crystal Sea at some point in the afternoon. We made our way over hills, through heavy brush, and across creeks. It took us several hours of non-stop, hard walking, but we finally came to a clearing at the bottom of a range of small mountains.

Valcor stopped us at that point. He showed me the front side of the mountain in front of us and told me that just one mile on the other side of that mountain laid the Crystal Sea. I was excited about the prospect of getting a chance to see the area where my great grandfather had his battle against the beast.

Then Valcor said, "We are close to reaching the sea and should be there soon. But I need to warn you about a potential problem along the way." I thought to myself, *Great! Another problem. What else is new?* Valcor continued, "All across this range of mountains lives a tribe of creatures called the Maltoids. The Maltoids were exiled to this area by the beast because they chose not to follow his plan of domination."

"Good. That means they're on our side...right?" I asked.

Valcor responded, "Not really. No one really knows where the Maltoids stand in the conflict. Even though they rejected the beast, they never came to us to join our side either. Travelers who have visited us after coming through this area have told tales of vicious creatures attacking them, sometimes severely injuring them or even killing others. Apparently the Maltoids don't like strangers to bypass through their territory, whether the strangers are good or bad."

So we made our way to the base of the mountain range and carefully began our walk up the mountain. It hadn't been long while on the mountain when we encountered our first Maltoid. The creature was my height. It was black and dirty. Its appearance reminded me of some of the old pictures my mom showed me of some of our ancestors who worked in the coal mines of Virginia. It had a rock in one hand and something like a snake in its other hand. I couldn't quite tell what it was holding, but whatever it was, it was alive and moving, wrapping itself around the Maltoid's hand and wrist.

Once we noticed the Maltoid, we all froze in our places, hoping not to give the impression we were aggressive towards it. The Maltoid stood there, just looking at us with its red eyes. Its appearance was creepy. Immediately I thought of what one of my aunts would constantly say to me when she visited, "You can't judge a book by its cover and you certainly shouldn't judge a person by their appearance. If there's one thing I've learned in life is that since

God doesn't judge our outward appearance but our heart, then I shouldn't judge anyone either." So even though I wanted to assume this creature was evil, I decided it would be wise to allow it to display its true intentions.

The Maltoid raised his arms and began moving them in a wild manner. All of a sudden hundreds of Maltoids came out from everywhere. They came from behind trees. They came from under rocks. They came from out of the bushes. Just about anywhere a Maltoid could hide there came one out of hiding. We found ourselves quickly surrounded and outnumbered.

Valcor turned to me and told me not to panic. Then Valcor shouted a command to all of us to form a tight circle and to prepare for battle. I quickly suggested to Valcor, "Let's not do that just yet. Why don't we attempt to speak to the Maltoids? If we form a battle circle they may interpret that to be a sign of aggression and think we mean them harm." Valcor thought about it and then agreed to do as I suggested.

Valcor called out to the Maltoids' leader. Their leader stepped forward. Just like all the other Maltoids, it had a rock in one hand and a snake-like creature in the other hand. Then it spoke, "State your purpose. Why have you entered our territory?" Valcor explained who we were and why we were on the mountain.

After Valcor's explanation, the Maltoid leader looked at me and asked Valcor, "So this human child is the one you speak of?" It walked over to me and got real close to me. I wanted to run because I didn't know what to expect. Plus, there was the issue of that snake-like creature crawling around the Maltoid's arm and wrist. That was just creepy to me.

"What's your name, human?" the leader asked me.

I said, "My name is Abigail."

The leader then spoke with skepticism when it asked, "Are you the chosen one our prophecy speaks of?"

I wasn't sure how to answer that question. If I said yes it may try to kill me. If I said no, our group could get attacked by all the Maltoids. If I said that I didn't know, I could lower the confidence of our group in me. So I said hesitantly, "Yes, it is as you say."

"We shall see," said the Maltoid leader. Then the leader looked at Valcor and stated, "Before we allow you to trample on our mountain, I must know for sure if this is the chosen one. Let's go to our camp to discuss how this will happen." So Valcor looked at me with a look to ask if I was comfortable with that idea. I nodded my head in approval and we headed to the Maltoid camp.

After a short hike halfway up the mountain we entered the Maltoid camp. I quickly discovered why they were so filthy and black. They lived in tunnels under the ground. Their camp contained numerous holes in the ground and as we walked past one of those holes, Maltoids would rise from them like groundhogs in the desert.

We came to an open area just on the northern side of their camp. There were rocks that lined the outside of that open area. Right in the middle of the open area was a deep hole with a long tree trunk running across the top of the hole.

The Maltoid leader then stopped at the open area and began to explain what was about to happen. It told us that in order for all of the Maltoids to know for sure that I was the chosen one sent to restore the harmony to their land, I would have to fight. I thought to myself that I could do that. I had already fought through a lot so I figured I could handle one of these creatures. Then the leader went on to explain in further detail that I was not fighting just one of their fighters, but two. These two were the very best fighters of the Maltoid camp.

Then an even scarier twist was added. I had to fight these two fighters while standing on the tree trunk above the hole. The leader went on to explain that the hole was bottomless. I didn't like the sound of all this. Valcor jumped in to defend me when he said, "The human cannot do as you say."

The Maltoid leader then pronounced, "If she can't fight then all of you will die immediately."

Valcor spoke back, "Let me fight instead."

But the Maltoid was insistent that I had to do the fighting. It responded to Valcor, "What are you afraid of? If this human is who you say she is, then she will survive. The prophecy speaks of one who will deliver us from the evil in our land. If the human dies in this fight, then her death proves she was not the chosen one. Now either let her fight or die."

I told Valcor that I would do it so he reluctantly stepped backwards. I made sure I had my staff with me and I slowly walked out to the center of the tree trunk. On each side of me walked out a Maltoid. Each one held a rock in one hand and a snake-like creature in the other hand.

All three of us stood there, waiting for the other to make the first move. It was a difficult situation for me because I could not see both of them at the same time due to their positions. If they both came at me simultaneously then I would be in deep trouble. As we stood there, I looked down and all I could see was darkness. My foot slipped slightly, sending a piece of the bark from the tree trunk down the hole. It went out of sight and I didn't hear it hit anything. That sent my anxiety levels way up. There was no room for error at this point.

Suddenly, the Maltoid to my left came closer. I turned to face it. Then the other Maltoid behind me came closer. I quickly turned to face it. Then they both came violently closer, flipping and screaming while remarkably keeping their balance along the way. They both came within a few feet of me. I acted on my first instinct. I stuck out my staff to where it was even on each side of me. Instantly, each Maltoid hit the ends of the staff, sending them flat on their backs. They both then retreated a few feet backwards.

Then the Maltoid on my left threw its rock, hitting me in the back of my head. I felt very dizzy and almost lost my balance, but my staff braced itself against the tree trunk and held me upwards long enough to regain my focus. Just then the other Maltoid threw its rock at me. My staff acted quickly and knocked the rock away before it struck me.

Both of the Maltoids began speaking to their snake-like creatures. Then they lowered their snake-like creatures to the tree trunk and the crawling creatures came towards me extremely fast. I didn't like snakes and I became petrified of the idea of those crawling things touching me.

As the snake-like creatures got close to me, they crawled under the tree trunk and out of my sight. I didn't know where they were. Then I felt a burning sensation on my left calve. I looked down and saw one of those creatures attached to me and wrapping its body around my leg. Then I felt the other creature biting my other leg and wrapping itself around my other leg. The pain was incredible. Not only were they biting me but they were also squeezing with intense strength.

Suddenly I felt them pulling me downwards. They had used their tails to anchor themselves to the log and were using that as leverage to pull me off the log. I knew what they were going to do. They were going to pull me off the tree trunk and once they had me suspended in the air, they were going to release me into the bottomless pit. I had to do something but I didn't know what to do.

I could not resist their strength any longer. I fell to my knees. As I did, my staff bounced out of my hand and rolled to the side of the tree trunk. My staff was caught by a few limbs on the tree trunk but it was out of my reach. I did the only thing I could think of. I grabbed the tree trunk and held on with all my strength.

Apparently the snake-like creatures had shot venom through me when they bit me because I could feel some strange things happening. I was having a hard time catching my breath and I was losing the feelings in my hands, which made it even more difficult to hold on to the tree trunk. At this point I felt desperate. The doubts began coming back in my mind. What if I wasn't the chosen one? I guess I was going to die and I would never see my family again.

By now I was on my stomach trying to grasp anything I could to hold on, but the creatures that were pulling me were too strong. My hands began to slip and my body began to slide. I could feel myself moving to the edge of the log. I noticed the two Maltoids jumping up and down with excitement. Then I took one last glance at Valcor. I looked at him as if to say I'm sorry for leading him to believe I was the chosen one.

My hands and arms had become entirely numb by this point and I could not hold on any longer. The creatures pulled me completely off the tree trunk, suspending me in mid air above the bottomless hole. I could do nothing to stop them. Then they did exactly what I thought they would do, they released me and I dropped down into the bottomless hole.

As I was falling, I was face up so I could see the tree trunk as it got smaller and smaller. While looking up I noticed a flash high above the tree trunk. The flash got bigger and bigger until it went past the tree trunk. It was coming straight for me. Then I noticed that the flash was not just a flash. It was the unicorn. The same unicorn that brought Chelsea and me to this land was flying towards me. Quicker than my eyes could keep up with it, the unicorn flew underneath me in the bottomless hole, catching me on its back.

The unicorn hovered for a few moments as I recovered from the venom of the snake-like creatures. The unicorn licked me on my forehead and instantly I had been healed from the venom. As we floated in the air, the unicorn spoke to me for the first time. He said, "Hi Abigail. You are the chosen one and I will not allow you to think anything less of yourself. I am here to protect you and assist you to fulfill your purpose."

I spoke back, "Thank you for saving my life."

The unicorn replied, "We need each other, Abigail. None of us could fulfill our purpose if we tried to do it on our own. Anyway, you will soon be saving my life and the lives of all the land."

"I'm feeling much better now. What did you do to stop the venom's effects?" I asked.

The unicorn responded, "One unique thing about a unicorn. We have the gift of healing. The creator gave us this ability by applying our saliva to whatever needs to be healed."

Like a jet we flew straight upwards right for the tree trunk. As we got to the tree trunk the two Maltoids looked at me with amazement. My entire group started shouting with joy. The unicorn flew me around to the front of the tree trunk. As he prepared to drop me off onto the tree trunk the unicorn said to me, "Now go take those two Maltoids down."

As I landed on the tree trunk, Valcor shouted with joy, "The human is the chosen one." Then all the other Hubearians shouted the same.

I reached down and grabbed my staff. My staff said to me, "Let's get 'em." The two snake-like creatures rose up and came for me with incredible speed. But as they both came within striking distance of my staff, I instinctively struck them both on their heads with the end of my staff, knocking the unconscious. Then I used my staff to flip the both of them in the bottomless hole.

Next, I slowly lifted my head from watching those two creatures fall out of sight and turned to the two Maltoids on each side of me. I said to them, "Let's dance boys." At once they each reached down and snapped off a limb from the tree trunk. Then they came for me. I learned from the first time I couldn't fight both at the same time while only facing one so I decided to try a new fight tactic. I stood with one shoulder facing each Maltoid and looked forward. Out of the corner of each eye I was able to see each one simultaneously. Once they came close enough to strike me with their limbs, I lunged at each one with each end of my staff.

I was able to hold each one off at the same time, blocking all their advances. Also, I struck blows to each one consistently until they backed off out of frustration. At that moment I heard the leader of the Maltoids say, "She *is* the chosen one!" His statement caused a panicked look on the faces of the two Maltoids on the tree trunk.

Once again they came running at me. This time, just before they reached me, I drove my staff into the tree trunk and catapulted myself over one of the charging Maltoids. Now I had both of them in front of me, gaining the momentum. I confidently charged the both of them, striking each one across their faces. They both flew backwards, with one landing on its side and one landing on its front. Both were unconscious.

There was a complete silence from the Maltoid camp. Then the leader shouted to me, "Finish them!"

I thought for a few seconds and responded, "No. I will not kill them. Let them live." No one had ever spoken back to the leader in such a manner. By this time each Maltoid on the tree trunk were waking up and discovering their leader had given the order to have them executed.

The Maltoid leader just stood there looking at me with a stunned look. I turned to the two Maltoids on the tree trunk and offered my hand. One grabbed my hand and the other grabbed the Maltoid reaching for me. I pulled them to their feet and told them to leave the tree trunk because the fight was over. I was choosing to let them live.

Then I spoke to the Maltoid leader, "These two are your best fighters. We need them to overcome the beast and his evil army. And, we need all of the Maltoids to join us in doing that."

"Your wish is our command, chosen one," the Maltoid leader said back.

I walked off the tree trunk to the congratulatory arms of Valcor, Tabukoo, and the rest of my friends. Tabukoo said to me, "You did it, Abigail. You did it. I knew you could."

Then I said back, "Thanks Tabukoo. But now not only do you know that, but so do I."

Then the unicorn joined our group, along with the Maltoids. All together we spent the rest of the evening at the Maltoid camp to prepare for the next day's journey, hopefully finally reaching the Crystal Sea.

The Croaksnakle

Early as the sun was rising on the next morning, we all got up and prepared to make our way to the Crystal Sea. After eating breakfast and packing our stuff, we began hiking up the mountain. After a short time of hiking we reached the top of the mountain.

Valcor stopped and told me to come to his side. When I reached him, Valcor said, "Abigail, look out in front of us."

When I did, I was amazed at the beauty of what I saw. Before me was a vast wilderness with a beautiful body of water right in the middle. I asked, "Is that the Crystal Sea that I have heard of so much?"

Valcor replied, "Yes it is."

The sea was memorizing from this distance. The sun's light glistened off the sea like a large piece of crystal. With astonishment I spoke, "No wonder you have named it the Crystal Sea. It reminds me of the crystals I saw in your cave. It is very clear, very bright, and very beautiful."

"Not only is the sea very beautiful, but it's also very mysterious. Many stories have been told about the sea's power. Still to this very day there is so much we do not know about it. Let me just tell you this. When we reach the sea, listen to me, don't go off by yourself, and respect the sea for what it could do." I listened intently to Valcor's instructions and tried to prepare myself for a day full of adventure.

We then picked up our pace, heading for the Crystal Sea. It wasn't long until we found ourselves standing within a few feet of the water of the sea. The sea's waves were gently crashing against the shore, much like a lake in my hometown. But this wasn't an ordinary lake like the one in my hometown. This sea was absolutely beautiful and completely clear. Even as I stood at its shores I could see for a long distance out in the water, even to the bottom most of the way.

Valcor shouted out to all of us to take a short break to rest. But then he stated to make sure we didn't go off alone and didn't go too far. Of course some did not listen, particularly some of the Maltoids. Several of them ventured out of sight. During our break I stayed close to Valcor, Tabukoo, and the Maltoid leader who I now had come to know as Grainus.

All of us slowly stepped to the water's edge, scanning the shore line and the water itself. It seemed that all of us had a watchfulness about us as we just didn't know what to expect. As we were standing there, Valcor began to tell me a little about the epic battle my great grandfather had with the beast. "Much of your great grandfather's fight with the beast happened in this same area," Valcor told me. "In fact, legend has it that the rock sticking out the water in front of us is where your great grandfather tricked the beast in trying to use his magic."

I just stared at the rock with amazement and appreciation for its history. As I looked closely at the rock I noticed at the tip of the rock it looked like it was blood stained. I wondered if that marking could actually be from the battle my great grandfather fought. Just as I was about to ask Valcor about the stain, we heard a loud cry for help. The cry for help came from the Maltoids who had wondered off and out of sight. So we ran as fast as we could in the direction of the scream.

The shoreline was bending and winding, making it hard to follow. We came to one area of the shore that bent around large rocks, making it impossible to see to the other side of the rocks until we actually got around them. When we did make it around the rocks we found only a few of the Maltoids. They were frightened to the point of being in shock. Grainus was able to calm them down over a period of a few minutes.

While we stood there waiting for the Maltoids to regain their composure, I happened to look out in the water. As I looked I noticed the surface of the sea off the shore was being churned like a tub of homemade ice cream. I thought that seemed out of the ordinary but in this land I could never tell anymore what was ordinary and what was not.

Grainus finally calmed down the Maltoids to ask them what had happened. One of the Maltoids could muster only one word, "Croaksnakle!" When he said it all of us felt a jolt of fear run through us. Then the Maltoid said it again, "Croaksnakle!" This time when he said it he said it with terror in voice.

Tabukoo said, "It's obvious that these Maltoids encountered the Croaksnakle at this sight. If they did this, that means the croaksnakle is probably still close by. I would suggest we get these Maltoids on their feet and get out of here as quick as possible."

Just as Tabukoo finished speaking I heard a noise behind me. I turned to see what the noise was and saw three slimy, squid looking things coming out of the water and sticking to the land, as if to surprise whatever they were trying to catch. I attempted to warn the Hubearians and Maltoids behind me but it was too late. The squid looking things had already grabbed two Maltoids and a Hubearian, pulling them out to the open water, and under.

Valcor then shouted, "It's the croaksnakle! Run away from the edge of the water, now!" Instantly, the croaksnakle rose from the water, making that terrifying sound I had heard while in the cave. Over and over it made that sound, sending chills all over me. The croaksnakle was huge. It must have been over twenty-five feet tall. It was moving too fast to count but it must have had at least a dozen arms that it used to grab its prey. And it was snatching Maltoids, Hubearians, and Tabukoo's friends all around me.

Not only was the croaksnakle huge but it was terrifying in appearance as well. It had a large mouth lined with extremely large teeth, shaped like a great white shark's teeth but much larger. Rows and rows of teeth filled its mouth. The croaksnakle's eyes were three in number and solid white. All over the croaksnakle's body were scars, slime, and suction cups.

I watched as the croaksnakle waved its arms around wildly, shaking each one of its victims until they became unconscious. Once one of its victims went unconscious, the croaksnakle would devour its victim…head first!

We were all running around in different directions attempting to flee from the presence of the croaksnakle. I looked in front of me and saw Tabukoo get snatched by one of the croaksnakle's arms. Instantly I rushed to his defense. By the time I reached Tabukoo he had already been pulled in waist deep water. I began pounding on the croaksnakle's arm with my staff, hoping I would inflict enough pain to cause the croaksnakle to let Tabukoo go. It was a terrifying experience.

Tabukoo attempted to speak to me through all the chaos of screaming and the croaksnakle's sounds. Tabukoo said, "Abigail. Let me go. There's nothing you can do for me now. You are too important to the future of our land to be caught by this croaksnakle. Now run while you have a chance." His advice was tempting because I was scared out of my mind. But I could not leave my friend. In the back of my mind I began remembering the bible verse my mom taught me when I was little. It had something to do with love and how there could be no greater love than when someone lays down his life for another. This was my chance to demonstrate that love to Tabukoo and the rest of our group.

As I continued to beat on the croaksnakle, the croaksnakle grabbed me with another of its arms and yanked me into the sky. My staff fell out of my hands and into the water. I quickly found myself, along with Tabukoo and the others, being swung violently in the air by the croaksnakle. The croaksnakle would submerge us under the water and then bring us out of the water. I was beginning to get weak from the impacts of being thrown against the water's surface. The Maltoids left on the shore were throwing their rocks at the croaksnakle to distract it, hoping the croaksnakle would drop us.

Slowly the croaksnakle began to descend under the surface of the water. I felt like there was nothing I could do but pray for a miracle. Strangely, however, I did not worry about my life this time. While facing the reality of death, I focused on my assurance that the Creator had a purpose for me and dying in the arms of the croaksnakle was not that purpose. I knew I had fought bravely and had tried to save my friend's life. I just felt like something was going to happen to free us of the croaksnakle's stronghold.

I was now being taken completely under the water. On shore I saw Valcor and the others watching as I went out of their sight. Right before I went completely under I grabbed one last large breath and waited to see what would happen next.

Deeper and deeper we went until, even in such clear water, I couldn't see but just a glimmer of light. Then, off in the distance, I saw what looked like a huge school of fish swimming towards us. Whatever I saw, it was approaching us rapidly. Then as it got in close I could tell that it was a school of fish…sort of.

The heads of these swimming creatures looked like a fish but their bodies had the shape of a beaver. They quickly encircled the croaksnakle in large numbers. Then they began swimming in circles around the croaksnakle, creating a whirlpool action. This caused the croaksnakle to spin in circles.

Faster and faster we went until the croaksnakle let all of us go. We instantly charged for the surface of the water, gasping for breath as we broke through. After gaining my senses, I grabbed another breath and stuck my head under the water to see what was happening. The fish creatures were pounding the croaksnakle by ramming themselves into the body of the croaksnakle. Each time they did this, the croaksnakle would moan until it finally swam out into deep water and out of sight.

Then the fish creatures headed for all of us. I raised myself out of the water and told everyone to swim to shore as fast as they could because we were not alone in the water. I did not know anything about these creatures, and I wasn't going to stick around to find out. I swam as fast as I could for land. Before I knew it the creatures had caught up with me. Their fins were sticking out of the water and close to my side. I decided to give up trying to beat the creatures to land so I stopped where I was.

Quickly they surrounded me in the water. I saw Tabukoo and all the others surrounded as well. Then I noticed a red fin coming straight for me. It was different than the rest, as the other fins in the water were greenish-blue. The fin came within a few feet of me and stopped. The fish creature then raised itself upwards in the water, like me, and it began to speak to me. The creature said, "Hello, Abigail."

I was astonished that it knew my name. I asked, "How do you know who I am?"

The creature said, "We all know who you are. Your name has traveled all over our land, and in my case, water. There has been a buzz of excitement all over about the possibility of the chosen one being with us. When my scouting army heard the croaksnakle earlier, we figured it had just caught another unexpecting creature. But with the possibility of the chosen one being in the area we decided to investigate for ourselves. It's a good thing we did."

"I don't understand. Who are you and what are your intentions?" I asked the creature. The fish creature responded, "Forgive my manners. My name is Bractus and I am the leader of the Aquaithians, which are these creatures before you now. We have come to escort you and your friends back to land."

I certainly was glad to meet a friendly face after all that I had just gone through. Two of the Aquaithians swam under each of my arms and swam me to the shore line where Valcor was waiting. I told Bractus thank you for his help in assuring our safety. Bractus, along with the other Aquaithians, then raised themselves up and out of the water. They stood there on their hind legs, using their tails to support themselves.

While we all stood together, Valcor invited Bractus and the Aquaithians to join us in our mission. Bractus accepted, but was only limited to action in the water. However, Bractus assured us safety from the croaksnakle anytime we came to the sea. Then, as quickly as they appeared, the Aquaithians disappeared back into the sea.

I looked at Tabukoo and smiled with a sense of relief. We all gathered ourselves and headed back to the spot at the Crystal Sea where we were before all this happened.

The Crocophants

Valcor determined that it would be best if we made camp for the rest of the evening since we had been through such a traumatic experience. So we found a site away from the shore and pitched our tents.

As the evening wore on, we built a big campfire for warmth and sat around plotting out our next day's travels. Now that we had arrived at the Crystal Sea we knew that we were halfway to the location of the beast. Our goal was to get there and destroy the beast before the other side could free him.

But we had a stop to make along the way. We hadn't forgotten about Chelsea and knew we had to rescue her before we reached the beast. If we didn't, Rapator and his evil gang would kill her in retaliation for us killing the beast. So we began formulating plans on how to rescue her.

Once we finished our plans, we headed for our tents to hopefully get a good night's sleep. Little did we know we were being watched from the water. If I had thought about looking to the water before I entered my tent, I would have seen countless beady eyes staring at us, waiting for the right time to attack. About ten yards out from the shoreline was an army of crocophants waiting for us to go to sleep. Crocophants were ugly creatures controlled by Rapator. The reason they were called crocophants is because they looked like a crocodile but had the size of an elephant. Rapator had sent the crocophants to prevent us from going any further in our travels.

These creatures were very patient, waiting several hours until the last one of us were asleep. Once the crocophants felt confident that they could spring their attack of surprise, they began to swim to the shore. Slowly and quietly they crept out of the water and onto dry land. There were about thirty in number and they did not enter our camp until each one had made it to land. Once the last crocophant had exited the water, they formed a plan to attack us from all angles, cutting off any routes of escape. Ten formed a shape similar to a half moon on our backside to prevent any retreat to the water. Another ten formed the same shape to our left and front. The final ten formed around our right and front, consequently making a circle around our camp.

Usually after a long and hard day like I had just gone through I would sleep really well. But for whatever reason I couldn't sleep that night. As I turned to my side to get comfortable I noticed a shadowy image outside my tent. It was the figure of a huge creature that I did not recognize. I immediately sat up and looked to my other side. There was another image on the outside of my tent on that side as well. Something inside me said this was danger approaching. My first thought was to run out of my tent and attempt to make it to the warning bell we set up in the middle of camp. But I wasn't sure what was outside my tent. So I grabbed my staff and carefully peaked outside my tent opening.

When I looked outside I was petrified at what I saw. It seemed the crocophants had positioned themselves strategically around our camp to enclose us in their attack. If I didn't do something and do it fast, there would be only one outcome after tonight...total destruction of our group.

I looked around at how each one of these creatures moved. Although they were big and scary, they moved awkwardly. I felt I could use my agility and speed to move through them to reach the warning bell. So I quietly opened my tent just enough for me to slip out unnoticed. First I slid my staff out on the ground and then I moved myself out of my tent. I grabbed my staff firmly, found what I thought was the best route to the bell, and I took off.

As soon as I moved, all heads of the crocophants turned to me. Instantly the closest crocophants to me attempted to stop me. One crocophant snapped in my direction, almost taking my head off. But I was able to see his strike coming for me just in time, bending backwards to allow his mouth to go right over my body.

Then I rolled to my right to escape the reach of that crocophant. As I did, I rolled right under another crocophant. It attempted to crush me by stepping on me. Each time it stepped I moved out of the way, barely dodging each crushing step. Finally I used my staff to knock two of its legs out from under it, hoping to knock it off balance to give me a chance to escape. My move backfired as the crocophant lost its balance but began to collapse on top of me. With every ounce of strength I had, I moved quickly from its gigantic body as it fell to the ground.

Dirt and debris flew up in the air, effectively blinding me temporarily. As I stood there in a cloud of dust and my eyes hurting from the debris that had lodged in them, I could hear the crocophants moving around me. Somehow I was able to compose myself and focus my hearing on each one. I had unknowingly developed sonar ability. I could see with my hearing. In my mind I could picture each creature as it positioned itself for the kill.

From behind me I envisioned one of the creatures coming for me. So I instantly turned and swung my staff for its nose, striking the creature. It immediately fell to the ground. By this time all the noise had awoken Valcor, Tabukoo, and all the others. I could hear all the chaos of my group engaging the crocophants. While hearing all this I was still able to focus on the surrounding crocophants. My eyes were still in tremendous pain and were now beginning to water to wash the debris out of them. But my hearing pictured in mind the location of each crocophant around me, as well as the warriors from my camp.

One crocophant charged me from my right side. I began swinging my staff in a windmill manner, and as the crocophant came within striking distance, I drove my staff directly into its right eye. The blow brought a halt to its progress and dropped it to the ground.

The first crocophant that I had struck jumped back up and lunged for me. I jumped and used my staff to catapult myself off its head sending me to its backside. It swiped at me with its armored tail but I was able dodge it. In my mind I saw the campfire next to me. I used my staff to flip a flaming piece of wood into the air and hit it towards the crocophant like a baseball player swinging for the fence. The fiery wood entered the roaring mouth of the crocophant, setting it on fire. It then made a hasty exit for the water.

By this time my eyes were beginning to clear up enough to where I could see again, although a bit blurry. I was trying to clear my vision as Valcor came out of nowhere and grabbed my arm, just pulling out of the way of falling crocophant that had been kicked by the unicorn. "Thanks Valcor!" I said.

He quickly replied, "Abigail, keep your head together. You can't lose focus one second." I understood his anxiety.

Valcor and I stood back to back as we faced off with the crocophants. Out of the flying debris I saw the mouth of a crocophant coming straight for me. Out of instincts I held my staff vertically to block the bite of it. The crocophant pressed against my staff. The pressure was tremendous. Somehow I was able to stand against it. As it moved closer and closer to me, I felt my arms growing weaker and weaker. The crocophant had made its way to within one foot of my face. Its teeth were ferocious. Its breath was horrible. I could see all kinds of flesh in its mouth between its teeth. I'm sure its plan was to make me its next meal.

My mind raced with ideas of how to stop the advance of the crocophant. As I was about to become a quick snack for this huge creature, my staff spoke to me. It said, "Lower me and duck fast." I didn't understand the instruction but

I did what it said. Unknowingly to me, the crocophant had moved me from the back of Valcor to the destructive flames of our campfire. I did what my staff instructed, allowing the momentum of the crocophant to carry it directly into the campfire.

In the distance I saw Tabukoo fighting against one of the crocophants. The crocophant had pinned Tabukoo against a large boulder. With my staff in hand I ran to the bolder, grabbing some rope along the way. I climbed it, reaching the point where I was directly above Tabukoo. I then hurled myself to the back of the crocophant. While balancing myself on the back of the massive creature, I wrapped the rope around the mouth of the crocophant. Just like the crocodiles from my land, this crocophant did not have the strength to open its mouth once tied shut. Then Tabukoo and I were able to bring the creature down.

Out of the dark came a crocophant from behind me. It grabbed hold of my shirt and flung me twenty yards backwards. I hit my head against a stump, sending me into a dizzied state. I couldn't regain my composure. I felt the ground shake and could see the crocophant charging me but there was not anything I could do. I was stunned by the toss and could not defend myself. As the crocophant came close, Grainus jumped between us, attempting to protect me from the charging creature. He fought bravely, holding the crocophant off me. I was about to gain enough of my composure back to help him when the crocophant snatched Grainus in its jaws, snapping him in two like a toothpick.

I screamed at the top of my lungs, "No!" The croco-phant then came for me. Right before it reached me, the unicorn flew in from the side, delivering a fatal blow to the temple of the crocophant with its horn. "Quick, Abigail, jump on my back!" the unicorn said. So I jumped on and he flew us above the camp. He allowed me to regain com-plete composure. As we hovered above the camp, I was able to witness the locations of each crocophant and dis-cern the momentum of the battle.

It was my opinion that we were losing the battle. We had defeated a few of the crocophants but they were so massive that it took several of our guys to fight one of them. We were suffering many injuries and some deaths. I had to do something but I wasn't sure what. Then the unicorn mentioned, "Abigail. I don't know if you know this or not but a croaksnakle's favorite food is crocophant." The unicorn gave me a crazy idea. What if we could somehow lure the croaksnakle to camp? Would it actually help us by driving away the crocophants? I knew I had to do some-thing so I asked the unicorn to fly us to the open sea in search of the croaksnakle. I wondered what Valcor and rest thought as they saw me fly off with the unicorn.

With tremendous speed the unicorn flew us around the sea in search of the terrifying croaksnakle. After about an hour of searching we finally found it. The croaksnakle had surfaced many miles from our camp. The unicorn told me to hold on and it flew us to the croaksnakle. We flew around it to get its attention. The unicorn repeat-edly kicked the croaksnakle on its head, making it angry. The croaksnakle wildly threw its arms at us attempting to knock us out of the sky. The unicorn was able to dodge each swing. Finally we felt the croaksnakle was so angry with us that it would follow us anywhere. So the unicorn began flying just above the water's surface and towards our camp, with the croaksnakle right behind us.

We finally reached the shore at camp and the croaksnakle was in hot pursuit after us. The croaksnakle was actually coming out of the water, right to the shoreline. I ran as hard as I could back to camp and into the raging battle. When I entered I was horrified to see Valcor being knocked around by two crocophants. I went to help him. As I reached Valcor, one of the crocophants swung its tail, knocking me away from Valcor and separating me from my staff. The creature then charged at me, pinning me against a rock. It stood there, just looking at me as if it were enjoying the moment before it ate me.

Then it opened its mouth and just as it started to hurl itself at me, a large squid-like arm grabbed the crocophant, stopping it in its tracks. It was the croaksnakle. The croaksnakle had grabbed the crocophant and yanked it straight up in the air and out of sight. Immediately the croaksnakle grabbed another crocophant…then another…then another.

Fear swept through the crocophants. Each one began to take notice of the croaksnakle. I looked to the shoreline and saw the croaksnakle waving several crocophants in its arms, devouring them one by one. The momentum had swung instantly in our favor. With the crocophants' attention on the croaksnakle, we were able to gain the advantage. I organized our guys into a formation that prevented the remaining crocophants from retreating to the woods. They had nowhere to go but back to the water.

Each one of us grabbed fiery torches from our campfire to herd the crocophants to the shoreline. The croaksnakle then picked them off one by one. As we got closer to the shore, we enclosed our formation. This made the crocophants head right for the croaksnakle. It was like a buffet for the croaksnakle. We were basically feeding the terrible creature with a number of other terrible creatures.

The croaksnakle grabbed each crocophant like candy off a shelf until there was only one crocophant left. The croaksnakle then began heading for the open sea, leaving the one crocophant. As the croaksnakle headed out of sight by going under the water, the crocophant turned to us. It stood there deciding whether to enter the water or give it one last try to fulfill its mission. But it admitted its defeat and headed to the water. As it got a little ways in the water, the croaksnakle surprised it, pulling it under. Then there were none. The croaksnakle had effectively eaten all the crocophants and helped us defeat our enemy on this battle. After battling the croaksnakle the day before, it had now become our ally.

All the Hubearians and the gang began cheering as they realized we had survived another intense battle. Valcor approached me and said, "When I saw you fly off with the unicorn I thought that maybe you were running from the fight. Not that I could blame you. But when I saw you return with the croaksnakle right behind you, I thought you had condemned all of us. I thought there was no way we could survive against the crocophants and the croaksnakle. But you had a plan, didn't you?"

I replied, "Valcor, your battle for this land is now my battle also. I would never leave you. But I did have a plan. Actually, the unicorn and I had a plan. The unicorn brought to my attention about the croaksnakle's appetite for crocophants. My plan was to lure the croaksnakle here so it could feed on the crocophants, essentially saving us from the crocophants. I just hoped the croaksnakle would cooperate...and it did."

Fortunately for us the croaksnakle did cooperate. But then again, that's how it is around here...one day some-one can be your enemy and the next your ally. I still don't completely understand all of what's happening, but I am starting to learn to trust in the Creator's purpose for me. Many times the Creator's promise of my purpose is the only unchanging thing around me.

The Memories

The next day we set out for the frozen land which imprisoned the beast. Valcor told us that if all went well, it would take a good seven days to reach our destination. However, we all knew from our past experiences that it was a very small chance that all things would go well. Before we could reach the frozen land, we had to make a stop along the way. Chelsea needed to be rescued and we all had a feeling deep in the pit of our stomachs about the difficulty of that task.

As we departed from the Crystal Sea, thoughts of my best friend filled my mind. I remembered how we first met. My family had been living in our Florida neighborhood for years. I was the fourth generation of my family to live there. Then one day during the hot summer of 1997 I was out in my driveway bouncing a basketball with my dad when I noticed a new family moving in the vacant house across the street from us.

That old house had been for sale for almost year, sitting empty while cobwebs grew on the inside and the landscaping grew out of control on the outside. The street I lived on was a quiet street with many families without children living on it. The only kid I knew on my street was a bully in high school. I longed for someone to play with that I could see each day.

Then Chelsea and her family arrived. They showed up in a big U-haul moving truck and a beat up mini-van. When they pulled into the driveway, I hoped there might be a little girl my age to play with. As I watched them get out of their vehicles, I saw her mom and dad get out first. Then her two brothers followed. I can remember watching them get out and with each person I grew more discouraged. Then, like people rejoicing after seeing the sunshine after a year long rain storm, I rejoiced when I saw Chelsea step out of the mini-van. I can remember telling my dad, "Daddy, daddy, there's a girl! Daddy, there's a girl!"

In no time we were playing together and it didn't take long for us to become best friends. As we grew older, we shared everything with each other. We even became blood sisters. You know what that is, right? Blood sisters are what you become with each other when you gently cut yourself on the palm of your hand and shake hands. This allows the blood of your best friend to mix with yours, creating a bond that can never be broken.

At age three we shared our first pizza together. At age four we shared our first ice cream together. At age five we shared our first movie at the theater together. At age six we shared our first football game together. At age seven we shared our first scary movie together. At age eight we shared our first summer vacation together. At age nine we shared our first emails together. At age ten we shared our first ride in my dad's new jeep together. At age eleven we shared our first boy crushes together. At age twelve we shared our first experiences playing fast pitch softball together. At age thirteen we shared our first experiences at having the same horrible teacher for math.

We started becoming really close when we played together in the summer of 2000. We visited local theme parks, recreation centers, museums, movie theaters, and local swimming holes. It seemed like every day I was either spending the night at her house or she was spending the night at my house. What a special summer that was.

Then the following year our friendship was tested. Chelsea's dad was diagnosed with cancer and not given much time to live. It was a devastating blow. As you can imagine most of her time was spent with her dad while she still had the chance to do so. Chelsea's dad lasted a good five months after being diagnosed with cancer. The day when he died was probably the hardest day of my life and I know it was for her.

After her dad's death, Chelsea didn't want to play much. In fact, she didn't want to do much of anything. She was like this for a long time and we went many weeks without even talking. I thought that I might lose her as my best friend until one day her mom came to me. Chelsea's mom asked me if I could come over for Chelsea's birthday party. Chelsea's mom told me that I was the closest person to her before her dad's death and I may be the only one that could bring her out of her depression.

On the day of Chelsea's birthday, I showed up at her house with a gift. We shared cake and ice cream, played silly games, and she even laughed a little. But those few laughs were all the joy she could muster at the time. I stayed after the other kids left the party. We spent a lot of time talking about her dad. That evening she cried on my shoulder until she couldn't cry any longer. Chelsea felt so depressed because of the loss of her dad.

All I could do was hold her and cry with her. Then I began sharing our memories together. Soon she was thinking about all we had done together. Then she began reflecting on all the memories she had of her dad in those times we spent together. An amazing thing began to happen. Chelsea began smiling and laughing as she remembered how her dad had been instrumental in introducing us to one another. One particular memory Chelsea had of her dad was when he dressed up like a woman to help us throw a tea party for our girlfriends. "He actually made a pretty woman," I said. Chelsea laughed. That was the turning point to Chelsea's recovery. That year we learned just how special we were to one another.

It was the following spring that we played at the neighborhood park for the first time together. I can remember how I showed her around the massive piece of land. Our park is a big open field with swings, slides, and all kinds of other contraptions that make up three different playgrounds. Our park also has an area where people let their dogs play with other dogs. There's a softball field, football field, and soccer field.

Of course there are trees, lots of trees. But there's one massive shade tree at the center of the park. It seemed that this particular shade tree was a favorite for most of the local neighborhood families. Over the years the shade tree became a symbol of perseverance and stability for all of us.

In the summer of 2003 we almost lost the shade tree. The neighborhood group that watched over the quality of life for our neighborhood came up with a bright idea of cutting down the shade tree to make room for a swimming pool. The idea of having a swimming pool to go to every day seemed inviting but a swimming pool could not replace what the shade tree offered all of us who played in the park day after day. Each day all the neighborhood kids would gather under the tree for not only shade but also to socialize with everyone else. The shade tree had become a gathering spot for all of us as we grew older. That old shade tree grew on each one of us. It had become a special place for all of us, especially Chelsea and me. The shade tree had become a place of shelter and peace for Chelsea after the loss of her father. Many times I would find Chelsea sitting at the base of the tree just because she needed to feel good about herself. It seemed that whenever we sat underneath the protective branches of the shade tree that life became so much easier. Later in life we come to understand exactly how special this tree was.

Each autumn created a buzz of excitement for Chelsea and me because that was the time that the shade tree turned colors. During the spring and summer the shade tree produced a large amount of green leaves. It seemed more than anyone could count. But it was autumn when the tree turned magnificent in color. The leaves on the shade tree would turn some of the most brilliant shades of red, yellow, and orange. It was almost like the tree was on fire because it glowed with majesty. None of the other trees in the park could even come close to the beauty of the shade tree.

The summer of 2004 brought another scare for us. We almost lost the shade tree to a fire because while barbequing in the park, an individual lost control of their fire when the wind blew some of the flames onto the picnic shelter. The shelter quickly took ablaze. The fire spread fast because that summer we were experiencing a drought. When Chelsea and I heard about the fire, we ran with all our strength to the park. Our deepest fear was that the shade tree would be gone when the fire was over. All three playgrounds had been destroyed by the fire and even one of the fields had been burnt up. But there stood the shade tree, tall and majestic as usual. Somehow that tree survived the fire without so much a burnt mark.

That old shade tree had helped Chelsea and me get through a lot of ups and downs over the course of time. It meant the world to us. I guess the tree itself represented Chelsea's and my friendship with one another. The tree had stood tall for many years, survived near tragedies, and given hope and love to many people. Chelsea and I could relate to that tree.

After all Chelsea and I had been through over the years, both good and bad, I think 2005 presented our toughest challenge. It was in that year that Chelsea thought she was going to move back to her home state of North Carolina. Chelsea's mom had been working hard trying to keep the family together since her dad's death. Then her mom received a job offer from a hospital in her hometown. The job was a good job. It offered her twice the salary she was making at the time plus the move would allow Chelsea's family to be close to her mom's parents. We just knew that she was going to move. I was devastated about the prospect of losing my best friend. We had experienced so many joys and sorrows together. I just couldn't imagine life without her.

One afternoon we both sat under the shade tree to talk about her possible move. We both were depressed because it seemed like everything was working out for the move to happen. While sitting under the shade tree, we both felt a sense of peace and acceptance come over the both of us. The shade tree was doing its magic again. We had spent so much time worrying about the situation and just in a short time the tree had brought calmness to us.

Chelsea told me that they were planning on moving in two days and she needed to tell me goodbye now because she wouldn't be able to have the strength to tell me when they leave. We told each other our goodbyes and hugged each other so tight that we couldn't breathe.

Chelsea's mom drove up to the park. We saw her get out of her car and we wondered why she was coming to us. Chelsea's mom walked over to where we were sitting. She knew how close we were and how hard this move was on the both of us. Chelsea's mom just stood under the shade tree and looked up in its branches. She mentioned that now she could see why we thought the world of the tree. Then she looked at the both of us and smiled. Chelsea's mom then proceeded to tell us that the job in North

Carolina had fallen through and they were not going to move after all.

Both Chelsea and I began crying with joy. We felt like a weight had been taken off our backs. Our prayers had been answered. We jumped up, screamed with excitement, and gave Chelsea's mom a great big bear hug. She began laughing with the two of us and mentioned that even though they would have been closer to family, she was glad not to move. Once again the shade tree had come through for us.

Chelsea and I had become inseparable over the years and now it looked like we would continue to be that way for a few more years. Chelsea was not only my best friend, but my blood sister. We were sisters as far as we were concerned. We had built so many memories while growing up together and I was not about to leave her behind in the hands of the evil Rapator.

The Ravine

As I thought about Chelsea and the memories we shared, I grew more determined in my spirit to rescue her, at all costs. I asked Valcor where we were headed and Valcor told me that in order to reach Chelsea we were going to have to cross a ravine. The ravine in itself was dangerous because it was two miles deep with sharp rocks at the bottom. Plus, the ravine had no bridge so we were going to have to find a way to cross it.

Valcor then told me that the ravine, even though dangerous, was not the most dangerous aspect to consider while crossing it. First, living in the walls of the ravine were small lizard like creatures that with one bite could kill anyone with its poison. Then if we make it across the ravine we likely would have cat-like monsters waiting for us. Then Valcor said with sarcasm, "Oh yeah. I forgot about the large birds that patrol the ravine looking for prey." I thought in my head, *Just another day at the office.*

After a short time of walking we reached the ravine. It looked massive. It must have been fifty to seventy-five yards wide and as deep as I could see. A strong gust of wind seemed to blow every few minutes. I wasn't fond of heights so this was going to be perhaps my greatest challenge. I just kept telling myself that the Creator had a purpose for me and it was not to fall to my death in this ravine.

We spent a while patrolling up and down the sides of the ravine to find the best place to cross. About half a mile north from our beginning point, we spotted what seemed to be a decent crossing point. Valcor had an idea to use the unicorn to fly him and some ropes to the other side of the ravine. Once on the other side, Valcor could tie off the ropes to some large trees a few yards beyond the ravine's edge.

A couple of the Maltoids tied three of our ropes to three separate trees on our side. Then Valcor gathered the loose ends of the ropes, climbed on the back of the unicorn, and both the unicorn and Valcor flew to the other side. After making it safely, Valcor took the loose ends of the three ropes and tied them to trees near him. The side of the ravine that Valcor now stood on was shorter than the side in which we all stood. The plan was to use our staffs as braces and slide down the ropes to the other side. The ropes were pulled firm and tight.

Valcor shouted to start coming across. We started with a few Hubearians, followed by a few Maltoids. Tabukoo and his friends would have to take turns alone on the ropes because of their size and weight. Since Tabukoo and his friends didn't carry staffs they would have to grab the ropes by hand and slowly lower themselves down the ropes to the other side.

The first few Hubearians and Maltoids made it safely. Then one of Tabukoo's friends took his turn. He grabbed hold of the ropes with hands and stepped off the side of the ravine. His weight put a huge stress on the trees in which the ropes were tied to. We became worried if the trees were going to snap or not.

Tabukoo's friend slowly made his way down the ropes. As he was about halfway down the ropes we could hear screeches in the distance. Then out of nowhere appeared several large birds. The birds must have been five times the size of an eagle. Their talons were huge and very sharp. The birds had beaks that seemed pointed enough to ram right through a person's body. These birds began circling Tabukoo's friend. Valcor shouted to keep coming down the ropes. Tabukoo's friend was obviously nervous.

The birds continued to circle Tabukoo's friend. It was also obvious that the circle was getting tighter. The birds had a plan. Then one of the birds, like a dart, headed straight for Tabukoo's friend. The bird went beak first into the back of Tabukoo's friend, causing him to scream in pain. Next, the bird let go of Tabukoo's friend and flew into the sky. Then the bird landed on the shoulders of Tabukoo's friend. The bird squeezed tightly, causing its talons to penetrate the flesh of Tabukoo's friend. Blood poured from Tabukoo's friend's body. Then the bird attempted to fly upwards. It was obvious the bird was trying to fly off with Tabukoo's friend.

Tabukoo grabbed a large rock and threw it at the bird, hoping to knock it off his friend. The rock hit the bird on one of its wings but the bird held on to Tabukoo's friend. The jolt from the rock hitting the bird caused Tabukoo's friend to let go of the ropes with one of his hands. He then dangled above the ravine, hanging on with one hand for his life.

Two more of the gigantic birds converged on Tabukoo's friend. One clutched Tabukoo's friend's free arm in its talons. The other bird dug its talons in the left leg of Tabukoo's friend. Then all three of the birds began working together to lift Tabukoo's friend from the ropes. Another bird landed on the rope next to the clinging hand of Tabukoo's friend. The bird then used its beak to peck at his hand. Eventually Tabukoo's friend could not hold on any longer and let go. Once free from the ropes, all four birds worked together to hold Tabukoo's friend in the air. Then they flew off with him beyond the cliffs and out of sight.

Just like that he was gone. I felt helpless. We all felt helpless. He had become bird food. After a minute of shock, we realized that we had to cross the ravine quickly while the birds were focused on Tabukoo's friend. So one by one we began crossing the ravine. Tabukoo and the remainder of his friends planned on crossing last.

I was in the middle of the pack. Finally my turn came to cross. I cautiously placed my staff on top of the ropes and placed my hands on each side of the middle rope, grasping my staff. With a firm grip, I gingerly stepped off the ravine's edge. For a split second I hung there as if I was frozen. My heart raced and beat so hard I thought it may jump out of my chest. With Valcor's encouragement I slowly began the slide down the ropes.

When I was a little ways down the ropes, I noticed something was crawling along the top of one of the ropes ahead of me. Whatever it was it was heading straight for me. The closer I got to the creature the more it looked like a lizard. Then I remembered what Valcor had told us about the poisonous lizards living in the ravine's walls.

When I reached the halfway point on the ropes, I suddenly stopped. One of the trees from the higher side of the ravine in which we had tied a rope to had become loose and that leveled out one of the ropes enough to cause me to stop. So I hung there above the ravine. The lizard approached me and now was sitting on the rope within an inch of my hand. I yelled at Valcor about the lizard. He said to be very still because if I move quickly I could startle the lizard and cause it to strike.

Then more lizards began approaching me on the ropes. I glanced at the ravine's side and saw that there were so many lizards crawling on the ravine's wall that it appeared the ravine itself was moving. A large trail of these creatures were crawling on all three ropes and heading up the ropes. It appeared that they were more interested in crossing to the other side of the ravine instead of lodging their fangs into my body.

I watched as the creatures crossed above me on all three ropes. Then some of them began crawling down my arms and onto my body. Pretty soon I had these strange creatures crawling all over me. They were sliding through my hair, in my ears, under my nose, and across my mouth. I could feel them crawling up my pant legs and into my pockets. I could even feel them scratching my skin with their claws as they hung on to my skin while being under my shirt.

The creatures were very nasty looking. They were covered in black and gray scales. Their tongues were slimy and red. They possessed sharp claws and rows of pointy teeth. But not only did they look nasty, they felt even worse. It took every ounce of my being to stay still as they used their tongues to check out my body. I could feel them wipe their slimy tongues in my ears, up my nose, and all over my body.

It was obvious these creatures were exploring me in order to determine if I was a friend, enemy, or even possibly food. I just hoped they didn't decide they needed to sink their teeth into me. As they continued their parade across me and the ropes, I focused on Chelsea and the purpose given to me by the Creator. Because of what I knew I needed to accomplish, I was able to weather the storm. Finally, after what seemed forever, the lizard creatures finished crossing. I was able to feel the last one leave my body and I slowly turned my head to see them crawling along the ravine wall behind me. At that point Tabukoo was able to fix the rope, enabling me to finish my slide to the other side of the ravine.

After I made it across, the rest slowly and cautiously followed. One by one the Hubearians, Maltoids, and others made it across. Finally, all that was left on the other side were Tabukoo and his friends. Since Tabukoo was the leader, he chose to go last, sending his friends one at a time. Because of their size, much stress was put on the ropes. After the first of Tabukoo's friends made it across I could tell that the trees were already loosening at their foundations in the ground. I wondered if the trees would hold out long enough to get them all across.

But the trees were not our only concern. Apparently within the wilderness that existed on this side of the ravine lived terrible cat-like creatures that were big and mean. Several of the Hubearians and Maltoids that already crossed stood guard to protect the backsides of those helping the rest cross the ravine.

As the second of Tabukoo's friends was crossing, those of us who had made it to the other side of the ravine began hearing weird noises off in the distance behind us. These noises were like a combination of a growl and a popping sound. I had never heard anything like it before. Valcor called out, "It's the Cataramas. Be on high alert!" Valcor then explained that Cataramas were the cat-like creatures that he mentioned earlier. "Cataramas are vicious," he said, "these creatures hunt down their prey and rip them to shreds. They don't even kill their victims before they do it. It's almost as if they enjoy watching and hearing their victims suffer."

Deep down inside I felt a sense of anxiety beginning to build. I just knew we were about to enter another conflict. The problem was we still had a few of our guys on the other side waiting to cross. The sounds grew louder and louder so we knew the Cataramas were coming closer. We worked feverishly to get the remainder of our guys across knowing we were going to need everyone for our encounter with the Cataramas.

We had gotten all but three of our guys across the ravine when the noises made by the Cataramas stopped.

There was complete silence coming from the wilderness. We didn't know what to think. Privately we all hoped the Cataramas had decided to leave us alone and go somewhere else. For what seemed like an entire minute we did not hear a single peep from anyone or anything. So we focused our efforts on getting Tabukoo and his two friends across the ravine.

Suddenly, from out of the wilderness jumped the Cataramas. They catapulted themselves at us from over top of the brush and small trees. Each one landed on one of our guys. I saw around me seven Cataramas perched on the bodies of four Hubearians and three Maltoids. Each Cataramas was the size of about two tigers. They were white with black and brown striping over their bodies. They had razor sharp teeth that ran through their mouths. Their mouths were oversized, almost taking up their whole faces. Their legs were muscular and their feet were large enough to cover a Hubearian's entire head. Their tails were twice as long as a normal tiger's tail. Obviously their tails were used as a weapon to subdue its prey.

The group of us who were attempting to get the last of our group across the ravine continued at our task while everyone else engaged the Cataramas. Behind me I heard screams and yells. I could only imagine what horrors my friends were facing as they attempted to hold off the Cataramas so we could get everyone across.

Finally we had gotten all across the ravine except Tabukoo. In the midst of the chaos behind me, I had forgotten about how loose the trees securing our ropes had become. Tabukoo grabbed onto the ropes and began his journey to the other side. About a fourth of the way across I noticed a splash of dirt at the base of one of the trees across the ravine. Before I could say or do anything, the tree popped out of the ground. Tabukoo's weight pulled the freed tree off the ravine's edge, sending it down the ravine. Tabukoo quickly grabbed the remaining two ropes and watched as the free tree fell downwards, coming to an instant halt when the rope grew tight again from the tree supporting it on our side. Once the rope grew tight again, the free tree crashed against the ravine's side, smashing the tree in many pieces.

Tabukoo hung there in mid air on the remaining two ropes. He looked at me with a look of fear in his face. It was if he was saying, "Please help me and don't let me fall." While looking at him, I saw behind him two more splashes of dirt. The last two trees were about to come out of the ground. I yelled, "Tabukoo! Move now!" He immediately started towards us. Then both trees came flying out of the ground. Tabukoo and the two free trees went downwards and swung up against the ravine's wall. I yelled at Tabukoo to hold on. And then I yelled at those helping me to begin pulling him up. Our problem was that not only was Tabukoo heavy, but the weight of the two trees made it almost impossible to get him up.

As if our problems were not enough dealing with the Cataramas along with pulling Tabukoo up the ravine's wall, we faced something new. The large birds had decided to return for seconds. The birds headed straight for Tabukoo. Our only chance to save Tabukoo was to get him up the ravine wall before the birds could carry him off.

As we were pondering what to do, a knife made of stone scooted by my foot on the ground. One of the Hubearians had lost it in its battle with a Catarama. I instinctively grabbed the knife and instructed Tabukoo that I was going to drop it to him. He needed to catch it and use it to cut the ropes below him to allow the trees to fall. Losing all the weight from the two trees could possibly make him light enough for us to pull up.

So I dropped the knife to Tabukoo and luckily he was able to catch it with his left hand. As he started cutting the rope, he held in his right hand the tree that the rope was tied to jumped right out of the ground. I screamed to Tabukoo to grab hold of the left rope and let the other rope go. The free tree flew by Tabukoo, barely missing him. But the falling tree did take out one of the birds as it went by and scattered the rest of the birds.

We began pulling with all our might to get Tabukoo up the ravine wall. We were able to get him within ten yards of the top when we felt the tree behind us beginning to get looser in its grip of the ground. I knew we only had a few minutes to get Tabukoo up or we would lose him. It didn't help that Tabukoo had to wave his knife at the birds to keep them from him. Every time he swung his arm it pulled on us who were trying to lift him to the top.

Tabukoo got within five feet of the top when the tree leaned forward. We only had a moment to get Tabukoo up, so we pulled with all our strength. Then, the tree came flying out of the ground and towards us. We all jumped out of the way as the tree went flying over the edge. As I lay on the ground, my heart grieved with sorrow because

I just lost my friend. I felt like I had let him down. Then I heard, "Hey is anybody going to help me?" The voice came from the side of the ravine. I raced to the edge and looked down. Tabukoo had let go of the rope just in time to grab a rock embedded on the ravine's wall. I then instructed the unicorn to fly down and push Tabukoo from Tabukoo's backside while we extended my staff to him and pulled him up. My idea worked like a charm as we were able to get him up and over the edge to safety.

Our joy from rescuing Tabukoo was short lived as the sounds of battle roared from behind us. We quickly turned to view all that was happening. As I turned, I looked directly into the eyes of a charging Catarama. The Catarama hurdled a Hubearian and flew right at me. My reflexes took over as I ducked my head; just missing the Catarama's outstretched claws. As the huge cat-like creature went over me I extended my staff, hitting the Catarama on its stomach, catapulting the creature up in the air and over the side of the ravine. Not wasting any time, Tabukoo and the rest of us jumped up and engaged the remaining Cataramas by the side of our friends already in the deadly battle.

Creatures and objects were flying through the air all around me. We were in a violent struggle against creatures that had the strength to tear us to pieces and the meanness to not stop until either we were dead or they were dead, whichever came first.

Out of the corner of my eye I could see Valcor fighting a Catarama. I ran over to him to assist in his confrontation. As I ran up to the Catarama, it turned towards me and roared so loud that the force of its breath caused me to fall backwards. While lying on my back the Catarama pounced on top of me. It had all four of its feet around my body to keep me from crawling away. As it stood above me, saliva from its mouth dropped on my head. It slowly lowered its face to about twelve inches above my face. I witnessed Valcor and two other Hubearians come to my aid only to have the Catarama use its tail to sweep all three of them off to a distance.

It was just the two of us now. The Catarama looked at me with intent to kill. I thought to myself, *This time I'm a goner. I can't move. No one is close enough to stop this creature from tearing me to shreds.* Just as the creature started to raise its paw to strike me, it looked behind me and froze. I wondered what was happening. Then the Catarama lowered its paw and began snarling. The Catarama's actions freed me enough to allow me to turn my head and look behind me.

I could not believe what I saw. It was thousands of the toxic lizards. They apparently came from the ravine's wall. *Great,* I thought, *As if getting eaten by the Catarama was not going to be hard enough to deal with, I first must get bitten by all those venomous lizards.*

The lizards covered everyone in their paths like Kudzu in the state of Georgia. Before I knew it, the lizards had reached me. They covered me and swarmed over the Catarama. Words cannot describe the feelings I was having while these tiny creatures crawled all over me.

Oddly the lizards were not attacking me but only the Catarama. The Catarama was being bitten all over its body but I was not being harmed in any way. The Catarama in its struggle against the little creatures fell over to my side and I slowly rose to my feet. When I did, I saw all my group standing on their feet. Each one had the same amazed look on their faces as I did. The tiny lizards were only attacking the Cataramas and not any of us. It was as if they had come to our rescue to protect us from the cat-like creatures.

In just a few short moments it was over. All the Cataramas were lying on the ground dead. The small had conquered the large. Once the Cataramas had fallen, the lizards then returned to the side of the ravine in which they had come from. The last lizard to reach the edge of the ravine stopped and turned to look at us. For a brief time, it just stared at us. Then suddenly it was gone.

I think every one of us were in shock. One moment we were engaged in a battle against a strong and dangerous foe, the next moment we were rescued by tiny creatures for no reason at all. The Maltoids had the ability to understand the thoughts of some of the creatures that lived among rocks and mountain sides. One of the Maltoids told us that as the last lizard stood at the ravine's edge, it was telling him that the lizards had come to help the chosen one complete her mission. Apparently when they were crawling all over me while I hung on the ropes, they were able to discern who I was. As it turns out, they were friendly creatures with the hopes of their land being restored to the peace it once had.

As the Maltoid told us all this I just stood there in amazement. Once again death had been cheated. Just when it seemed I was going to suffer death, the Creator provided another way out. It was obvious to me that the Creator had a purpose for me. Even in my hardest times, I will never doubt that again.

The Valley

After regrouping from our conflict with the Cata-ramas, we set out for the bottom of the mountain known as Mud Valley. Valcor thought it would take us the rest of the day to reach the valley, so we took our time to allow all of us to rest our tired bodies. Shortly after dark we reached an open field about one hundred yards above the valley. There we camped for the night.

The next morning we packed our supplies and pre-pared for another day of travel. Valcor then warned all of us of the possible dangers that awaited us in Mud Valley. He told us that the reason the valley has the name Mud Valley is because of the mud that covers the basin of the valley.

All along the valley floor are pits of mud deep enough to swallow Tabukoo. Also there are reported frequent mud slides. These slides are what feed the mud pits. Then Valcor warned us about mysterious creatures that are rumored to live in Mud Valley. Valcor told us of stories from wayward travelers about how they witnessed creatures that lived in the mud. These creatures supposedly had the ability to live in the mud.

We cautiously entered Mud Valley, fully aware that there was danger around us. However, our purpose outweighed the dangers ahead of us. We stood just above the base of the valley and watched the mud activity. We could see many mud pits. These pits were large, deep, and boiling. They were almost like a boiling spring but instead of water they were of mud.

We took our time to decide on the best way to cross the valley. During our watch we didn't see any signs of mud creatures or even mud slides. We finally decided on what we thought was the best way to cross and prepared to set out on that journey.

Suddenly, underneath our feet, the ground began to shake. Then before any of us could react, the ground gave away. It was a mud slide. The bank on which we stood was now moving down with incredible speed. I could see below us a big mud pit. We were headed right for it and there was nothing any of us could do about it.

With incredible speed we hit the mud pit, sending mud all around us. Each one of us was caked in mud. I felt like a peanut in an M&M candy. Fortunately, not all of our group was caught in the slide. Those who were still standing on the bank above us immediately dropped their ropes to us. We grabbed the ends of the ropes and were pulled out of the mud pit to dry ground.

We sat there and looked at each other for a few seconds. Afterwards we all broke out in laughter when we realized just how muddy we were. As we were laughing, one of the Maltoids sitting next to me was suddenly struck in the back of the head by a large ball of mud, knocking him unconscious. We went from laughter to immediate silence.

As I turned in the direction from which the mud ball came, I saw several more heading for us. It took all I could do to dodge them. After the mud balls missed I was able to focus on three objects standing about fifty feet behind us. At first I wasn't able to figure out what those objects were. There was so much mud on my face that I was having a hard time seeing. Plus, the objects looked like giant mounds of mud themselves.

Through the mud on my face I could tell the objects were moving. Then I heard the sound of more mud balls forcibly flying by me and striking others sitting around me. Then I remembered! There are tales of mud creatures living in the Mud Valley. I wiped the mud from my eyes the best I could so I could see. There they were. Those three objects were giant mud monsters. Their appearance was like a huge mound of mud with arms, a head, but no legs. They seemed to glide along the mud in which they lived.

One of the creatures raised its arm to throw a ball of mud. The mud was hurled right for me. As it reached me I raised my staff, splitting the mud ball in two. We all quickly jumped to our feet and prepared to engage the muddy monsters. The others at the top of the bank could not do anything at this point but watch.

The three mud creatures approached us to within twenty feet. They stood in front of us, starring at us. Then without warning, they each began hurling mud at us. The force of the mud was tremendous, knocking all of us backwards. We hit the bank behind us and then fell to the ground. I thought to myself that this couldn't be happening. It was mud. How could mud be so hard to deal with? But the mud was so thick it was like being hit with a soft rock.

While we were all lying on the ground, the creatures prepared to throw more mud on us. I think their intentions were to bury us alive, or kill us from the impact of their throws, and then bury us. I wasn't going to let that happen. I quickly regained my composure, jumped to my feet, and held my staff in a defense position.

The creatures then sent their mud balls for me. Using my staff, I was able to deflect every mud ball. One creature came for me. Before I knew it, the mud creature was right in front of me. The creature grabbed me with its arms. I used my staff to knock its hands off me. When I did, my staff went through the mud, severing the creature from its hands. The creature backed up. It then looked at its arms. In just a few seconds, new hands formed from the mud on its arms. The creatures could regenerate because of the endless supply of mud around them.

Then the muddy hands on my body began to spread. The mud slid down my body until it reached the ground. There, the mud was able to gain a continuing supply to capture me. The mud spread quickly up my body. Every inch on my body covered by the mud was stuck. I could not move from my waist down. Then the mud began moving further up. I yelled for help. But the creatures began slinging mud balls at my friends around me, preventing them from helping me.

With each second the mud spread more and more. Finally the mud approached my shoulders. The only parts of my body free from the mud's paralyzing grip were my arms and head. I knew that if the mud was able to cover my face I would not be able to breathe. Time was running out.

Then the mud began covering my arms. Slowly it moved down my arms until my arms were covered all the way to the ends of my fingers. Next, the mud began creeping up my neck and heading for my head. Unfortunately by now I could not move anything on my body below my face. I yelled up to Valcor, who stood on the bank above me, "Valcor! Get a rope to the unicorn and have the unicorn fly down here to place one end of the rope around me. Then have the unicorn pull me up to where you are. My only hope is to get out of this mud so the mud covering me will be cut off from its source." Then I couldn't say anymore as the mud covered my entire head.

I stood frozen, caked in a layer of mud, and it was suffocating me. I could not breathe. My only hope was that Valcor and the unicorn heard me. Then, I felt something fall on me and grip me tightly around my waist. Suddenly I could feel like I was being pulled upwards. However, the mud around my feet was strong and didn't want to let go of me. After a few seconds of struggling, the mud broke and I went flying upwards. At this point I couldn't see because of the mud and was losing consciousness because I couldn't breathe. Then, all things went black.

The next thing I knew, the blackness began to lighten up. I could hear voices in the distance of my mind. The voices were calling my name. "Abigail! Abigail! Abigail, wake up! Wake up Abigail!" The darkness became even lighter until things around me became fuzzy. I felt myself opening my eyes. My eyes opened to the sight of Valcor, Tabukoo, the unicorn, and others standing above me. They were all looking directly at me.

I spoke, "Where am I?"

Valcor told me they had pulled me from the mud and tore the shell of mud off me in order to help me breathe. Apparently they rescued me just in time.

Once realizing that I was going to recover, Valcor and the unicorn rushed to the rescue of the others still trapped in the onslaught of the mud creatures. I couldn't do anything but slowly regain my strength and senses as the others were pulled to safety.

After everyone was rescued and we regained our composures, we began rethinking how we were going to cross the Mud Valley. It was evident that the mud creatures were too powerful for us to defeat them. We had to out smart them to get across.

It was obvious to us that the mud creatures could move freely among the valley because they had so much mud to rely on. And after being down in the mud we knew the mud was extremely warm, allowing the mud to move like a fluid. Our only chance was to somehow figure out how to cool down the mud and thereby slowing down the mud creatures, making them ineffective.

Valcor then remembered about the flying dragons from the north. These dragons were different in that instead of breathing fire they could blow cold breath. Valcor seemed to think that the dragons' breath might be cold enough to at least slow down the mud to give us a chance. The dragons from the north were the answer to our dilemma. However, the dragons poised another question. How would we get them from the north to where we were?

Tabukoo recommended that I ride the unicorn to the north to locate the dragons and bring them back to Mud Valley. Fortunately, the unicorn knew how to find the dragons. But no one knew if they were even friendly or not. The dragons were our only hope at this point so I hopped on the back of the unicorn and we took flight.

The Dragons

After a long time of flying, I could sense we were approaching the northern part of the land because the air was rapidly dropping in temperature. Ahead of us I could see what looked like snow capped mountains. Then, snow began falling all around me from the above clouds. We were definitely getting close to the dragons' territory.

While flying, I saw movement in front of us. It seemed like two objects in the distance were rising into the air from a far distant mountaintop. The closer we got to the objects the higher they went, until the objects were at our level.

The two objects in the sky began to take shape the closer we got to them. Like a light turned on in a dark room, it suddenly hit me what the two objects were. They were both dragons. Our approach into their territory had put the dragons on high alert. They were attempting to intercept us in mid air. The unicorn told me to hang on tight as we approached the two dragons. Neither dragon looked happy to see us.

I had in my mind before actually seeing them what dragons were supposed to look like. But these dragons were not anything like what I expected. They were not that big. Each dragon was different in coloration. One was a cream color with black and silver markings while the other dragon was a light blue-green color with red and dark green markings. Even though they had different colors, they were similar in other ways. They both had the same shape. Each dragon was longer rather than wider and each was around nine feet in length. Both dragons also had long tails that ended with circles on the tips of their tails. Of course they flew with their wings, which were longer than their bodies. These two dragons were beautiful but terrifying at the same time.

Both dragons hovered in the sky in front of us. The unicorn and I, once we got within twenty-five feet of the dragons, hovered in the sky as well. It was a tense moment. The dragons just hovered in front of us, not making any sounds. While we were focused on the two dragons in front of us, three more dragons approached us from behind. Suddenly, we were surrounded by five dragons. I was not sure about their motives, but it was obvious the dragons were extremely cautious.

The unicorn then turned to me and suggested that I attempt to speak to the dragons. I responded to the unicorn, "Me? Why me? I don't know what to say or even how to speak to a dragon. This is your land. Shouldn't you be the one to say something?"

The unicorn said, "I could say something. But you are the chosen one. You have the authority to command these dragons to listen. I am just a unicorn."

So with that logic I looked at the two dragons in front of us and mustered enough courage to open my mouth. "Greetings, we come in peace," I said to the dragons. "We have flown from the Mud Valley in search of help."

The dragon with the red markings quickly interrupted me when he said, "What business is it of ours? We are not interested in the Mud Valley. All we care about is why you have entered our territory unannounced."

I spoke back by saying, "We have traveled from the Mud Valley in hopes we could receive your help."

The dragon with the silver and black markings then responded, "You have made a very dangerous decision to come here like you have. Others have come our way unannounced and have been frozen in ice or simply torn to shreds. What gives you any idea that we would want to help you?"

The unicorn then told me that now would be a great time to introduce myself. I nodded to the unicorn and nervously said, "My name is Abigail Parker. And I am the chosen one who will free your land of the evil that is spreading across it." At that statement, all five dragons started laughing.

"You, the chosen one? You are just a little human girl! How can you do anything about the evil in our land?"

I said, "Believe me, I have asked myself that same question many times. But all I know is that my great grandfather, Jonathan Parker, came to your land a long time ago and defeated the beast. Now I am here to finish the job. I am not sure how but I know the prophecy speaks of the first girl born in Jonathan Parker's family coming to this land to rid the land of the evil, and I am her."

A purple and yellow dragon from behind blurted, "You said your great grandfather was Jonathan Parker?"

I responded, "Yes."

The dragon with the red markings then said, "Jonathan Parker was a friend of ours. We are the ones who helped put the beast in his icy tomb. Jonathan was a great man who had a noble heart. If you are who you say you are, then the time of redemption for our land has arrived. We would be willing to help you if you are the chosen one. But first we must know for sure."

When the dragon stopped talking, all five dragons immediately blew their frosty breath at us. The unicorn bucked me off its back and straight up in the air. While I was in the air, the unicorn became frozen solid, immediately dropping to the snowy ground. As the unicorn fell downwards, I fell with him. All I had to brace for the impact was my staff. As I looked to the ground which was rapidly approaching, I saw nothing but deep snow drifts and I hoped they were deep enough to cushion our fall.

Both the unicorn and I hit the snowy ground hard. I went a few feet deep into the snow. The snow around me began caving in on top of me. Because I hit the snow so hard, I was compacted into the snow and could not move. My staff was still in my hands and pointing vertically, with the end of it above the top of the snow bank in which we fell in. I thought for sure this might be the end of me. I couldn't move, the snow was burying me alive, and there was no one to help me.

In just a few moments the snow had covered me completely. I was in the dark and could not breathe. Then I could hear movement above me. The next thing I knew something was pulling on my staff. My staff began going up. I held on with what strength I had left. Slowly I began to move upwards and through the snow. My hands then broke through the top of the snow, followed by my elbows. Finally my head popped through. I could breathe again and I gasped for air.

As I opened my eyes, I saw a little dragon maybe half the size of the ones I encountered in the sky. The little dragon was blue, orange, and black. It looked at me with the innocence of a child. I gained enough composure to ask, "Well, are going to just stare at me all day or are you going to pull me the rest of the way out of the snow?"

The dragon responded, "Oh, sorry." Then it pulled me out of the snow.

Once on my feet again, I looked at the dragon and told it thank you. The dragon then asked, "Who are you?" I told the dragon who I was and that I had come to seek the help of the dragons. Then I looked around for the unicorn. I saw the unicorn embedded in the snow about thirty feet away. I rushed to the unicorn and tried to free him from his icy prison, but I could not.

The dragon then flew over to me and asked who it was I was trying to free. I told the dragon about the unicorn and how he had been a loyal friend to me. The dragon then told me to step aside; that he could help. The dragon then blew what seemed like hot air on the unicorn, melting the ice that surrounded the unicorn. Soon the ice was gone the unicorn was able to move again.

I hugged the unicorn and asked how he was feeling. The unicorn said, "Good, I guess. Now I know how an ice cube feels."

With joy, I turned to the dragon and asked, "I thought you dragons could only blow cold air with your breath?"

The dragon responded, "We mostly do only blow cold air, but we can blow hot air as well. We just don't choose to use our hot air out of fear that Rapator will find out and force us to melt the ice away that holds the beast. But you seem like a nice creature so you won't tell, will you?"

I said, "Of course not. Your secret is safe with me. Thank you for helping me and my friend."

At that moment the other five dragons that had frozen the unicorn and sent both of us to the ground, landed next to us. The dragon with the red markings then addressed the little dragon that helped us, "Little Johnny, what have you done?"

Little Johnny answered, "What I have done is shown mercy. This human creature has claimed to be the chosen one. I'm not going to let her die in the snow. If she has come to help us, we can't kill her."

The red dragon said, "Johnny, we don't know if she is the chosen one. We have to test her to find out."

The little dragon looked at me and said, "She looks trustworthy to me. Can you think of any other humans around here?"

The other dragons looked at each other as if to say, "The kid has a good point." Then the red dragon spoke to me and asked, "You said you came to us for help. What kind of help do you need?" I informed the dragons of our situation at Mud Valley and explained our idea of using their cold breath to slow down the mud creatures enough to allow us to cross the valley.

After hearing my plea for help, the dragons decided to help me. "But first," the red dragon said, "we must share in our ritual of the battle meal."

I forcibly said, "We don't have time to waste! My friends are trapped at the Mud Valley. We need to go now!"

The red dragon then replied, "It is our tradition to share a meal together before we go into a battle. If we cannot share the meal then we cannot share the battle."

The unicorn and I agreed to share the meal because we knew the dragons were our only hope to get through the Mud Valley. We all flew to an icy cave in which the dragons made their home. Once inside, they started a fire with their breath. We all gathered around the fire. A green and gray dragon was instructed to gather the food for the meal. The dragon walked to a large box covered in dirt and picked it up, shaking the dirt from the box.

The dragon then walked over the fire with the box and opened the lid. Inside the box was a mixture of living and crawling bugs. These were not like any bugs I had seen back home, however. The dragon went from one dragon to the next, carrying the box, and allowing each dragon to pull out its favorite bugs to eat. I noticed that none of the dragons were eating. They were just holding the bugs in their claws.

I asked why none of the dragons were eating. Little Johnny told me that it was a tradition that when a first time guest was present, the guest had to eat the first bug. I thought to myself, *Great!* Finally, the box made its way to me. I looked inside the box and saw creepy crawlies in all shapes, colors, and sizes.

"Try the blue ones," said Little Johnny. So I grabbed a blue one. It was four inches long. The bug had antennas all over its body, along with several claws and more legs than I could count. The dragon with the box told me that I had to get more than one. He said this was a time of celebration. So I could eat all I wanted, like a buffet. Little Johnny recommended I also try the black and white bug as well as the orange and purple bug.

I told Little Johnny thank you for his help and said I think those three were plenty of food for me. Once all the dragons had selected their favorite bugs to eat, they turned to me to watch me eat my first one. The moment of truth had arrived. I told myself that what I was about to do had to be done for the creatures of this land. So I held the blue bug above my mouth, and while it was twitching in my fingers, I dropped it in my mouth. As soon as the bug went in my mouth, the dragons shouted in joy and began digging into their juicy bugs.

I could feel the bug in my mouth crawling on my tongue. I bit the bug in two, shooting green gunk out my mouth. It took everything I had to not vomit because I knew that if I did not eat these bugs the dragons would be insulted and probably not help me. I chewed reluctantly and then swallowed. I said, "Yum, tastes like chicken."

Little Johnny asked, "What's chicken?"

I said, "Never mind."

Without any of the dragons noticing, I secretly let my other two bugs go under a rock on the ground next to me. Meanwhile, the dragons finished up their gourmet meal. After the meal, the dragons blew out the fire and said, "It is time to fly. Thank you for sharing our battle meal with us. Now, lead the way."

I jumped on the unicorn's back and we took off out of the cave and into the sky. There were a total of seven dragons, including Little Johnny, which took to the sky and followed us. It was going to be a long flight back to Mud Valley. I was just hoping that we were not going to arrive too late to help.

The Rescue

After a long time in the air we began to approach Mud Valley. What I saw did not look good. The mud creatures were attacking Valcor, Tabukoo, and the others by slinging giant mud balls at them. Every time one of my friends was hit by one of those mud balls, they would be knocked unconscious. The force behind one of those mud balls was strong enough to kill a person if it connected in the right place.

Several of my friends had fallen down the banks and in the mud. The mud had caked my friends in a thick layer of gooey mud. My friends and I were in for perhaps the toughest battle yet simply because we could not get any kind of footing at the point of attack. Once we entered the mud valley, we were rendered almost completely helpless.

Valcor somehow had fallen down into the mud valley and was at the mercy of one of the mud creatures. Valcor was down on his knees as the mud creature swung its arm, striking Valcor and sending him several feet backwards hitting the bank. Valcor then slouched over and fell face down in the mud. As I witnessed this I instructed one of the dragons flying close to me to use his breath to cool down the mud creature which struck Valcor. The dragon inhaled and blew as hard as he could, freezing the mud creature right in its tracks.

When the rest of my friends witnessed the freezing of the mud creature, they all shouted in triumph. The sight of our return with the dragons encouraged everyone to fight harder.

Each dragon began blowing their cool breath on the mud creatures below us. The mud creatures quickly recognized us above them and they began hurling their mud balls at us.

During the heat of the battle, I had the unicorn fly me down to where Valcor was lying. There I was able to pick him up, out of the mud, and the unicorn flew us to the other side of Mud Valley. I left him there to recover and asked the unicorn to fly me back to action.

Tabukoo was defending himself from the onslaught of a mud creature. The mud creature was not only flinging mud balls at Tabukoo, but also shooting steady streams of mud at him as well. All Tabukoo had to defend himself was a large rock he had picked off the ground. In the middle of the fight, one of the dragons froze the mud creature. Then Tabukoo took his large rock and threw it at the frozen mud creature, shattering the creature into hundreds of pieces.

After seeing this, I instructed the unicorn to fly to each of the frozen mud creatures. My plan was to get close enough to the creatures, then have the unicorn kick the frozen mud creatures and breaking them apart.

We started carrying out my plan and it worked. The unicorn's kick was powerful enough to shatter the frozen mud creatures. We had just arrived at our fourth frozen mud creature when I heard Tabukoo yell, "Watch out!" As both the unicorn and I were looking at Tabukoo, the mud creature reached out and grabbed the back legs of the unicorn. Apparently the mud creature was thawing as we approached it and we did not realize it.

The mud from the mud creature slowly began moving up the body of the unicorn and was already approaching me. By this time, there was too much mud holding the unicorn for the unicorn to break free. The mud was now running up my legs. I knew I only had seconds before the mud would smother the both of us.

With my staff I swung through the grip of the mud creature, separating the creature from us. Then I told the unicorn to use every bit of strength it had to fly away. As we flew away, the mud continued to cover us but at least it did not have a source to keep coming from. We just barely made it to the other side of the valley when the mud reached the unicorn's wings, causing us to fall to the ground.

Because the mud did not have a source of mud to continue feeding it, the mud had to spread very thin to cover us. Little Johnny saw us covered in mud and flew to our rescue. He landed beside us and blew his cool breath on us, freezing the mud. But because the mud was so thin, the mud became like a thin sheet of ice on us and was easily broken off of us by Valcor.

As all four of stood on the other side of the valley, we witnessed the battle continuing in the valley. Dragons were flying in the sky. Mud creatures were shooting unlimited mud at them. Tabukoo and the rest of our friends were doing anything they could to survive the battle. It was complete chaos.

Then I came up with an idea. I asked the unicorn if he had enough strength to fly us to the dragons. The unicorn said he did, so off we went again. Quickly we were in the air in the same area of the dragons. I shared my idea with them. My idea was to have the dragons start cooling down the actual valley of mud itself instead of the creatures. To this point, the dragons were cooling down the mud creatures but as soon as one cooled down another one would rise from the valley. My thought was if we could freeze the source then it would eliminate any future mud creatures from forming as well as eliminate the source of the current mud creatures.

The dragons thought it was worth a shot and began blowing on the valley of mud itself. Over the course of the next several minutes the mud creatures began slowing down. The mud was hardening, preventing any future mud creatures from forming. My plan was working.

Soon the entire mud valley was as hard as a rock. The mud creatures had run out of a source to grow from. They were still attempting to throw mud balls but as they did they lost that part of their bodies. The more they threw the smaller they became.

Once the dragons were done freezing the valley of mud, they began working on the existing mud creatures.

One by one each mud creature became frozen until they were all frozen.

At last, we had overcome the mud creatures of the mud valley. My next order of business was to lead the rest of our group across the frozen mud valley to the other side before the mud thawed. One thing about the mud was that because of its warmth, it would not stay frozen long.

The unicorn flew me to the middle of the valley and I instructed everyone to follow us across the valley. Quickly we crossed the valley. As the last one made it to the other side, we could see the mud beginning to move again. We had made it just in time.

Once we all made it a safe distance from the mud valley, we all stopped to rest. All of the dragons landed on the ground where we were as well. We rested the entire afternoon because we were exhausted.

Later that evening the dragons suggested we celebrate with the sharing of a meal. I knew what that was like but how could I ruin it for everyone else? Valcor, Tabukoo, and everyone else were exited about the idea. So the dragons started a fire and then sent out to collect our celebration dinner.

Later that night we gathered around the fire and I shared with the dragons about all that had happened up to reaching Mud Valley. They were astonished at my tales of danger and adventure. Then they committed themselves to our cause of riding the land of evil. Unfortunately, the dragons had to fly back to their northern territory after dinner, but would assist us again if we needed them.

Meanwhile, the dinner itself turned out to be a traumatic experience in itself. Once we had all sat around the fire, a dragon took his collection of juicy and moist bugs around to each of us. It was funny watching the faces of each creature as they were presented with their choice of bugs.

Valcor was sitting next to me. As he looked in the bowl of bugs, I leaned over to him and suggested he try the blue ones because they were the best. Once he grabbed a blue bug I told him he should try the black and white bug as well as the purple and orange bug because they were not bad either.

Valcor looked at me and asked me how I knew how the bugs tasted. I just smiled and told him there is a lot about me that he did not know about yet.

Once all of us had gathered our favorite bugs in our hands, the dragons looked at Valcor. I explained to him how the dragons were waiting on him to take the first bite because it was their tradition to allow first time guests to eat first.

So Valcor did the unexpected. He took all three bugs and threw them all in his mouth at the same time. I could hear the crunching and popping in his jaws as he chewed the bugs up. He smiled at me as I watched him. When he smiled his teeth were full of body parts and guts. He had stuff hanging from his teeth that I had no idea what it was. All I know was it was nasty.

I could not help but laugh this night. After all we had just gone through; it was good to be able to laugh for a change. This was one of the most memorable evenings I had ever had. I will never forget it.

The Stream

We all took our time waking up the next morning. It seemed that each one of us were sore and had a hard time getting going. The Mud Valley experience had taken more out of us than any of us realized.

Tabukoo was busy stretching and Valcor was packing up his gear. I personally headed for the nearest stream of water to freshen up. There was a little stream just several yards outside of our camp.

Once I arrived at the stream, I dropped to my knees and bent over the water. I cupped my hands and filled them with water, splashing my face. This was my attempt to wake myself up because I was feeling extra tired this morning.

As I was kneeling over the stream, something in the stream caught my eye. I noticed it because the light from the sun was reflecting off the object. I reached in the water to pick the object up. It was an old pocket watch. Of course it was rusted and did not work. However, it was odd to me that a pocket watch would be in this land at all, especially in the little stream were I was kneeling.

While holding the pocket watch in my hand, I began hearing what sounded like people whispering. Immediately I looked all around me, but could not see anyone. Then the whispering stopped.

I looked back at the pocket watch and noticed it was made to be opened in the back. So I flipped it over and broke through the rust and mud to open the pocket watch. Inside the watch was an old black and white picture of my great grandmother. Her name was Abigail. I was named after her. I had only faint memories of her. She died when I was only five.

The interesting thing about my great grandmother she would always tell me stories of adventures she had with my great grandfather, Jonathan. Up until finding the pocket watch with her picture I always thought they were stories she made with her imagination, but I at that point I began connecting the dots and realized my great grandmother had come to this land at some point with my great grandfather.

What memories I do have of my great grandmother were good ones. I can remember always feeling protected and special when with her. It is strange to say but she made me feel like I had a future purpose or destiny. I can remember her telling me when I was sad to keep my head up because I was special. She would tell me that because I was special I would accomplish a special purpose one day. I always thought she was saying things like that because she loved me. Perhaps she also knew about the prophecy of this land. Perhaps she knew that since I was the first female born in the bloodline of my great grandfather that

I was the one the prophecy spoke of. Anyway, she always looked at me and spoke to me with pride.

I continued to look at the picture when the whispering began again. This time I stood to my feet and looked behind me deeply in the woods. Still, I saw no one. I yelled, "Who's there?" No one responded, but I was certain I was hearing people talk.

Frustrated, I turned back around, facing the stream. What I saw startled me. Across from me on the other side of the stream, stood my great grandmother...Abigail Parker. She was beautiful and young, just like in the picture I found in the pocket watch.

My first response was fear. I wanted to run but I could not. So I just stared at her as she stared at me. She looked at me with a smile on her face. Then she began to speak to me. She said, "Hello Abigail. Don't be afraid. I know seeing me after all these years, and in a way you never knew me, must startle you. But I have some important things to tell you."

At this point I did not know what to say or even if I could move my mouth to say anything to begin with. Then my great grandmother said, "Abigail...Now you know why I told you that you are a special child. From the day you were born I knew you were destined to come to this land, the land of the Crystal Sea, and finish the work your great grandfather left behind.

"Jonathan worked hard at making right what he messed up by coming to this place, but just could not finish the job. I returned to the land of the Crystal Sea many times with your great grandfather to help the creatures of this land adjust to their changes. While here I was able to learn about the prophecies of this land.

"Once your great grandfather and I discovered that the first born female of his bloodline would return to destroy the evil unleashed here in the land of the Crystal Sea, we looked to each birth of our family with great anticipation. As the years went by and no girls were born in our family, we both began to lose hope we would see what the prophecy calls the chosen one.

"In the last few months of your great grandfather's life, we found out that your mother was pregnant. Unfortunately, your great grandfather did not live long enough to see your birth. His loss was a big blow to me. If it wasn't for you coming along when you did, I may not have made it on my own."

I finally found enough courage to speak up. I asked, "So that's why you spoke to me about purpose and destiny so much?"

My great grandmother responded, "Yes, because your birth brought hope and aspiration to so many people and creatures, both in our land and in the land of the Crystal Sea.

"Your great grandfather and I looked for you for so many years. Then he died right before your birth. Your birth gave me new life and gave me a sense of purpose in my remaining years of life. I knew I had to pass on to you your calling without making your mind up for you.

"The land of the Crystal Sea celebrated for joy when you were born. Your birth brought a renewed sense of life to this land as well. The creatures of this land who wanted it to return to peace knew it was just a matter of time."

I then said, "It is amazing how things are coming together for me. As I think about my life, there were a lot of things that happened for a reason. It is kind of like my life has been made up of a chain of events, linked together, leading me to fulfill my purpose."

My great grandmother then said, "All things are connected. Our lives are not by chance. Now is your time to fulfill your destiny. All your life you were being prepared for this moment.

"But, Abigail, I must warn you. Don't let your guard down. Just as there are many creatures here in the land of the Crystal Sea who celebrate your coming, there are also many creatures who desire to destroy you. There is a dark evil in this land. That evil wants to control every creature of the Crystal Sea and rule them by an iron fist. You, Abigail, represent the only force that stands in their way of accomplishing their evil desires."

After hearing my great grandmother's warning, I said, "I have been through many fights and hurdles already just to get where I am now. I have seen great evil and know that there is a side of this great land that wishes I fail. The beast is my objective. I must destroy the beast. But I know Rapator will do everything in his power to stop me."

My great grandmother then warned me, "Don't just look ahead to Rapator, Abigail. There are those right in your own camp who wish you harm. In fact, there is a specific one who says they are supportive of you but secretly is plotting to kill you. Beware, and trust no one."

With concern, I asked, "Who is it that I can't trust?"

My great grandmother then told me, "Not even I know who it is who plots against you. Only you will find this out when the time is right. Just be ready and do not let your guard down with anyone."

As my great grandmother finished warning me, I heard the whispers from behind me again. I quickly turned around because I thought that there were people behind me witnessing my conversation with my dead great grandmother. But once again I found no one. I took just a brief minute to scan the woods. I even took a few steps towards the woods to help get a better look.

Once I found no sign of people, I kept looking in the woods as I began telling my great grandmother about these whispers I was hearing. Then I turned towards her while talking and saw that she was gone. Once again I was startled, but this time at her disappearance.

Suddenly, I began to feel like I was going to faint. Then, I passed out. The next thing I knew I was waking up with Valcor, Tabukoo, and some others standing over me calling my name.

Slowly I was able to wake up and they helped me stand. Valcor asked, "Are you alright, Abigail? What happened?" I told Valcor about my encounter with my great grandmother.

Valcor then asked me if I had drunk any of the water from the stream. I told him I had but asked what that had to do with anything. Tabukoo jumped in and informed me that the water from the stream has elements in it that makes a creature imagine images from their past.

"So you are telling me I imagined my great grandmother because of the water?"

Valcor said, "That is right. Your great grandmother must have had an impact in your life and the water caused your mind to imagine her and your conversation with her. This is why you passed out."

I said, "I have heard the expression of 'Do not drink the water' but this takes the cake."

Tabukoo said, "Well at least the good news is there are not any long term effects from the water so now that you have woke up you should not have any more imaginary conversations."

Then I remembered the pocket watch. I reached in my pocket where I had placed it. My pocket was empty. Then I asked if any of the creatures of the land of the Crystal Sea had ever met or heard of my great grandmother. Each one around me said they had never heard of her or met her.

Because of the absence of the pocket watch and my friend's testimony of never meeting my great grandmother, I felt like I needed to dismiss what had happened as a hallucination. However, the warning my great grandmother gave me stuck in my mind. I began wondering if there was someone close to me who could betray me like she said. As I looked at those around me, I felt there was no way any of them could do that. So, with confidence, I returned to camp with them to prepare for our day's journey.

Little did I know that if I had returned to the stream where I had been kneeling I would have found a small, round object half buried in the mud. The pocket watch which I supposedly had imagined was real. And if I had taken the time to go back to the stream and find the pocket watch, I might have noticed that off a few yards, hidden behind some limbs of a tree, was the spirit of my great grandmother. She watched as my friends walked with me back to camp. This time, however, she was not smiling.

The Captivity

On the same day that I was recovering from my encounter with my great grandmother, Chelsea was dealing with her captivity in the camp of Rapator. Before the beast's imprisonment in his icy tomb, the beast had taught Rapator on the evil magic. Now, Rapator used that magic often.

Rapator also had a reputation for mistreating his prisoners, and Chelsea was a reflection of his reputation. Rapator and his evil army had set up camp along an active volcano's base. Rapator loved the heat from the molten lava. The heat was used to torture any poor soul who was Rapator's captive. In this case it was Chelsea. Since her capture, Chelsea was often placed in the pit of the steam that came from the flowing lava. Rapator did this just because he liked to see her suffer.

On this particular day, Chelsea was bound at her hands and feet by a barbed plant that Rapator used to bring endless pain. The plant was called a barbed ruby flow plant. It got its name because when pierced by the plant, it caused blood to flow from the body. Rapator had one of his evil creatures take the plant and rap it tightly around the wrists and ankles of Chelsea. The barbs had pierced deep into her flesh, causing her to lose a lot of blood.

Chelsea was brought lunch that day and it consisted of a bowl of a wet rice-like substance and insect wings. Of course Chelsea refused to eat it, like she had been doing since her capture. By this time she was not only losing blood, but losing weight…getting weaker by the day.

"Come on, human, eat!" the guard said, "Don't you want to live?"

Chelsea ignored the guard and kicked the bowl against the cave wall, spilling its contents.

The guard said in disgust, "Humans are so stupid!" Then he walked away.

Later in the day, Rapator visited Chelsea where she was being held captive. Chelsea was in a small corner of the cave inside the volcano's base. There Rapator approached her. Rapator said, "What is the matter, Chelsea? Do you not like your living arrangements?" Chelsea refused to acknowledge him.

Then Rapator said, "You know, you are a lot like your great grandfather. He was hard headed like you." Rapator's statement roused the attention of Chelsea. She slowly looked up in Rapator's direction. "I thought that might get your attention," Rapator said. He went on to say, "Do you think your presence in our land is an accident? What's going on is not just about your pathetic friend Abigail. You have something at stake as well."

Chelsea then mustered the strength to ask Rapator what he meant by what he was saying. Rapator replied, "What I mean is that you also had a relative visit our land a long time ago. The only difference between Abigail's relative and your relative is your relative is still alive and present in our land."

Chelsea spoke back, "I do not understand. The only human presence in this land before Abigail and I arrived was her great grandfather and his best friend. When did my great grandfather come to the land of the Crystal Sea?"

Rapator then said, "Your great grandfather arrived at the same time as Abigail's great grandfather. Don't you get it? Your great grandfather and Abigail's great grandfather were best friends."

Chelsea said, "I do not believe you! You are a liar!"

Rapator jokingly replied, "Oh Chelsea. Don't say such things. You might hurt my feelings!" After a short pause, Rapator continued, "That is right, Chelsea. Your great grandfather is none other than the beast!"

"No! You are trying to trick me! There is no way my great grandfather could ever had been as evil as the beast! Never!"

With a smirk on his face, Rapator continued, "Oh he is the beast and I can assure you that he was…and still is that evil. You see, once your great grandfather tasted the power he had over the creatures of this land, he just could not refuse to embrace it. The greed, selfishness, and hunger for control and popularity just consumed him until he transformed into the hideous beast that he is today."

At this point Chelsea began crying as she listened to Rapator. All the emotions from her experience in the land of the Crystal Sea, from her missing Abigail to the anguish of her captivity, had finally gotten to her. Rapator went on, "Think about it, Chelsea. How did you meet Abigail to begin with? Your family moved in the same community as Abigail's family because your relatives had known Abigail's relatives for a long time. This is because Abigail's great grandfather and your great grandfather were best friends."

Chelsea then, through her tears, starred at Rapator as he continued. "One more thing to think about, Chelsea. Do you know what happened to your great grandfather?"

Chelsea asked, "What do you mean?"

Rapator responded, "I am asking if he died or not!"

Chelsea then answered, "Well, I do not know. I never met him because he was not around when I was born. I remember my grandmother telling me he had just mysteriously disappeared one day and no one knows what happened to him."

Rapator smiled and said, "I know what happened to him. He disappeared from your land because he never left this land!"

Chelsea just dropped her head in shame as she was able to put the pieces together. Chelsea realized that even though Rapator was evil and misleading, what he was saying had a good chance of being true because it all fit perfectly.

Chelsea then asked, "Why are you telling me all of this?"

Rapator then said, "Don't you get it? One reason is I just get a kick out of bringing you misery. The other reason is I want you to join my team and free your great grandfather."

Chelsea then said, "Are you serious? If what you say is true, that still has no bearing on me and how I live my life. What makes you think I would want to betray my best friend and betray the good that is in this land?"

Rapator looked Chelsea directly in her eyes and with a grin said, "Because it is in your blood. Your great grandfather faced the same decision and chose his own route. I think you will do the same."

Taking her attention off Rapator, Chelsea just stared off in the distance and began pondering all that she had just been told. She began questioning herself and wondering if she, like her great grandfather, was capable of doing such horrific things.

As Chelsea thought about their conversation, Rapator said, "Well, it looks like you have a lot to think about. Take your time, but do not take too long. Soon we will be heading to the north to free your great grandfather. I hope you are with us. I know he will be thrilled to see one of his relatives along his side. However, you do have to make that choice." Then Rapator left Chelsea by herself.

Chelsea felt numb all over her body. Suddenly the pain from the barbed ruby flow did not bother her anymore. All that was on her mind was how she was going to respond to what she had been told. She thought to herself, *Could all this be true? Could the beast really be my great grandfather? If so, does that mean that I will turn out like him and do evil things?*

Question after question rolled through her mind. She was in such shock and disbelief that she did not know up from down. She asked herself, "Is it possible that all my life has been a preparation to do evil? This is not the type of family business I imagined I would be in one day."

After thinking for a long time, she finally had come to a conclusion. She called for the guard to come to her. Once the guard arrived in front of her, Chelsea asked the guard to take Rapator a message.

"Go tell Rapator that I have made a decision. Tell him that I would like to speak to him immediately." The guard left Chelsea to find Rapator and deliver the message.

As she waited on Rapator's arrival, Chelsea thought back to all the good times she had with Abigail. She remembered the times they had snowball fights. Those were special days because it had only snowed a couple times in their life, while living in Florida.

Chelsea remembered the school plays they performed in together. Also the sports they played together. So many good memories she had of her and Abigail. She just could not imagine Abigail not being in her life anymore.

Finally, Rapator arrived. He asked, "You sent for me?"

Chelsea answered, "Yes. I have made a decision about what I am supposed to do."

Rapator stood in anticipation of Chelsea's decision. Chelsea knew what she needed to do.

The Dream

Halfway through our day, we took a break from our day's journey. Valcor told all of us to take a thirty minute break. Some gathered in small groups to talk. Others took a few minutes to eat. I, on the other hand, decided to use my break to catch a few winks of sleep. My body was still tired from our battle at Mud Valley.

So I looked for a comfortable spot to spread out. I found such a place a few steps outside of camp. There I found a rock to lay my head on and closed my eyes.

After what could not have been more than a few minutes I was awoken by a loud noise coming from the trees behind me. I quickly jumped to my feet to see what or who was behind me.

Before me stood a little creature in which I had not seen before. The creature stood about four feet tall and was muscular in shape. Its appearance reminded me of a Hubearian but was repulsive to look at. Its entire body was covered in long hair that was matted together by what looked like dried blood. I could barely make out a face behind all the hair.

The creature just stood in front of me, staring at me and not making any kind of sound. I was able to break the awkward silence to say hello to the creature but the creature did not respond back to me. Then I told the creature my name and asked the creature if it could understand me but still, no response from the creature. It just looked at me like a dog trying to figure out what its master is saying to it.

As we stood in front of each other, staring at one another, I heard a noise coming from behind me. I looked over my shoulder and noticed that a second creature was standing behind me. At this point I felt like I might be in some kind of trouble, so I yelled for help from Valcor and the others just a few steps away from me. Unfortunately, I did not hear a response. So I yelled even louder but I still did not hear any response.

The next thing I knew I had two more creatures on each side of me. Now, I was surrounded by these creatures. Once again I yelled for help. Nothing but complete silence filled the air. I wondered if maybe those in my camp just couldn't hear me.

Then, the creature standing in front of me raised his hand. Immediately, the other three creatures simultaneously rushed me. They knocked me to the ground and tied my hands behind my back.

Two of the creatures then lifted me to my feet. The creature standing in front of me then said to me, "You are coming with us." He then pulled a glowing turquoise rock about the size of a baseball from this pocket. He raised the rock above his head and a turquoise ray shot from the rock and made a large turquoise circle about five feet in front of us. At that point, one of the creatures walked through the turquoise circle and disappeared. Next, the two creatures on each side of me escorted me to the circle and together, all three of us stepped in the circle of turquoise light. Finally, the creature holding the stone followed us until all five of us had made it through the circle.

Once we made it through the circle, we entered a different land. On the other side of the circle was a desolate land. It was nothing like the lush, beautiful land of the Crystal Sea. I saw destruction all around me. For as far as I could see there was nothing living.

The creatures then led me about seventy-five yards down a slope until we came to a large, dead stump in the ground. The creature that appeared to be the leader then tapped a signal of thumps on the stump with a rock lying next to the stump. The stump then began to move. It moved and exposed what looked like a tunnel underneath the ground. We all then entered the tunnel one by one.

Inside the tunnel was a series of steps, like a stairway, that ran deep into the ground. In fact, the stairway of steps went so far I could not see the end. So we made our way down these steps.

Once we reached the end of the steps, we walked in a big, open space. In this space were many of the same creatures who had taken me as their prisoner. As soon as they all saw me, every one of the creatures stood up. Each creature looked at me with a look of sadness and desperation. Whatever had happened to them must have been terrible.

A door to my left in the tunnel wall opened. When it opened, all the creatures bowed to their knees, including the four creatures that brought me there. Through the door walked another creature. But this one looked older somehow. His hair was matted and dirty, just like the others. However, I could tell by the dryness and how the creature walked that he was older than the other creatures.

Whatever this creature's status was, I could tell he was well respected by the others. The creature walked over to me. I stood in silence not knowing what to expect. Then the creature opened his mouth and said, "Abigail." I recognized the creature's voice. It sounded like Valcor's voice. But there was no way this creature was Valcor.

The creature then ordered for me to be brought to his chambers by the four creatures that captured me. Once in his chambers, the other creatures left leaving just the one creature and me. He then asked me to sit down so we could talk. He then apologized for having to tie my hands but he knew that I would not have come with his escorts willingly. So he then told me was going to untie my hands.

The creature then continued, "Abigail, don't you recognize me? It is me, Valcor." I was in complete shock and confusion. I thought to myself, *How can this be Valcor? What in the world is going on?*

He went on to say to me, "I know you are confused right now. But I need you to listen to me. I am Valcor, the Hubearian that you know as your friend. You have been brought to this land by my Hubearian servants for a reason.

"First, let me tell you that you are still in the land of Crystal Sea. However, you are now fifty years in the future. The land is nothing like you know it to be in your time."

I interrupted the creature, "Wait! Wait! Wait! You are telling me that you are Valcor? You're the same Valcor who is the leader of the Hubearians...the same Valcor who trained me to fight with a staff...the same Valcor who encouraged me to keep my faith to accomplish my purpose?"

The creature responded by simply saying, "Yes."

I then continued to speak by saying, "So you are Valcor? And you are telling me we are now fifty years in the future from the last day I remember?"

Once again the creature responded by simply saying, "Yes."

I then began processing everything in mind and said back to the creature, "Give me a few seconds to think about this. If I am truly fifty years in the future, then was the land above the ground truly the land of the Crystal Sea?"

Once more, the creature simply responded by saying, "Yes."

I continued, "The four creatures that brought me here, brought me here through a ray of light. Was that the time portal that allowed us to get here?"

The creature graciously responded, "Yes."

Thinking out loud I went on to say, "I thought those creatures looked similar to Hubearians but their appearance was terrifying. They looked beat up and bloody, almost to the point of not knowing who they were. Valcor, what has happened to all of you? What has happened to the land of the Crystal Sea?"

Valcor began answering all my questions by telling me about the choice I made fifty years ago. Valcor told me that I allowed myself to become consumed with doubt and fear. He told me that I lost my confidence in myself and lost focus of what my purpose was.

After that, I chose to leave the land of the Crystal Sea and go back to my own land. Once I left, there was not anyone to stand against Rapator and the evil army he led. Most of the creatures of the Crystal Sea who wanted good to win gave up after my departure.

Valcor explained to me that he did all he could to stop Rapator with what creatures remained to fight with him but they just were not strong enough to stand against the ever growing power of the evil army.

Rapator became powerful enough to free the beast from his icy prison. Once the beast was released, the land began to be consumed with evil. What I saw above ground was the result of evil ruling the land unchallenged. Many of the creatures who stood in the beast's way were killed. Valcor told me that Tabukoo and the unicorn were both killed by the beast.

The Hubearians, the original protectors of the land's harmony, became a renegade of rebels who were forced to live underground. I found out that for the last fifty years the Hubearians had been living like this. They were all beaten up and bloody because of their never ending battle with the evil that existed above ground.

At this point I had to stop Valcor. I asked him, "So all that you are telling me is a result of me making a bad decision?"

Valcor replied, "Yes, it is. All our decisions, good or bad, have consequences that follow."

In my mind I just could not understand all of what I was hearing. I then asked Valcor, "Why did I leave the land of the Crystal Sea?"

What Valcor had told me up to this point was devastating to me. But what he was about to inform me went beyond devastation. I was in no way prepared to handle what came next.

Valcor said, "What I am about to say to you will come as a complete shock. You decided to leave the land of the Crystal Sea because someone close to you betrayed you, hurting you to the point of you giving up on your mission."

"What?" I said in disbelief. "I can't imagine anyone I know doing something like that."

Valcor continued, "The person who betrayed you was Chelsea."

Upon hearing this I fell to my knees and began crying. I just could not believe what I was hearing. "Chelsea is my best friend!" I cried.

Valcor told me about Chelsea's relationship with the beast. It was ultimately her relationship with her great grandfather that caused her to turn against her best friend. After all, my mission was to destroy the beast...Chelsea's great grandfather.

Chelsea's feelings about protecting her great grandfather led to her own transformation into a hideous beast. Valcor then said, "Once Chelsea became a beast like her great grandfather, you had to not only destroy her great grandfather but also Chelsea.

"All of that was just too much for you to handle. Like your own great grandfather who could not bring himself to kill his best friend, neither could you bring yourself to kill Chelsea. So instead of fulfilling your mission, you simply gave up and returned home."

At this point I was experiencing so many emotions I cannot begin to describe them. I thought that all hope was gone. But just as soon as I thought all hope was gone, Valcor gave me a new ray of hope. He told me, "Don't give up yet, Abigail. All is not lost. There is still a chance things can be saved. This is why I brought you here, fifty years in the future."

Through all my tears and heartbreak, I looked up at Valcor and asked him what I needed to do. He said, "You are being told this now so you have a chance to keep this future from happening. What you need to do is return to your correct time with the knowledge you have now. You must get to Chelsea before it's too late. There is still the chance you can keep her from making her choice to betray you and follow the beast.

This is our only chance to change what the future holds. I only have the ability to travel in time once, and now it is done. You get one shot to change things. If you fail, all is lost. Now, Abigail...don't give up. Please don't lose heart. You must stay focused on your mission and fulfill it. Remember, it is written in the prophecy."

After hearing Valcor speak his words of encouragement to me, I made the decision to not wallow in my sorrows and get up immediately. I knew that I did not have the time to feel sorry for myself. Not only did the future of the land of the Crystal Sea depend on me, but now the very future of my best friend rested in my hands.

Valcor's door leading from his chamber to the open room outside opened and he told me I must leave immediately. As I walked into the open room, all the creatures starred at me. I stared back. A little Hubearian walked over to me. The young Hubearian grabbed my hand and gently said to me, "Please don't give up. Help us." I took a good look at all of them because they reflected the bad decision I made in their past. It was then that I realized the blessing I was receiving. Not just anyone can gain the opportunity to see how life is effected by the decisions they make. I was one of the blessed ones to know how the future would turn out by just one decision. I never realized just how many lives are changed by our actions.

I then began walking up the stairs. The further I got up the stairs the darker it became. Finally, it became completely dark and I was not able to see anything. I yelled for help from the Hubearians. I needed them to show me the way out. But no one responded.

The next thing I knew I was waking up back in my own time, still laying in the open space I found earlier. I looked up in the sky and realizing where I was, I jumped up quickly. I was back in the same spot where I was when the Hubearians from the future took me through their time portal.

I pondered on all that I had just experienced and wondered if it was just a dream. I also remembered my conversation with great grandmother and how she warned me that someone close to me would betray me. I could not say for certain if what I had just experienced was a dream but I did know that I had a renewed since of urgency to rescue Chelsea.

The Dioxum

I ran back to our camp where I found everyone still resting. I located Valcor and rushed to him. When I reached him, I wrapped my arms around him and gave him a big hug, lifting him off the ground. He looked at me and asked, "What are you doing?" I told him I was just glad to see him and that I appreciated his kindness.

All the other creatures standing around us began laughing at us. But I did not care because I had a glimpse into the future. I had a snapshot of what was at stake for all of us.

While standing with Valcor, I asked him if we could cut our break short and continue on our journey. He agreed and ordered all the creatures with us to begin moving on. Again we were on our path to rescue Chelsea.

We had been walking for several hours. In fact, it was now beginning to get dark. We approached an area of large rocks surrounded by large trees. As we walked in the area we noticed there were skeletons lying all around us. The skeletons must have been from a variety of different creatures throughout the land.

We all stopped to examine the skeletons. As we got closer to the bones, some of the Hubearians with us recognized some of the bones to be Hubearian skeletons. Valcor looked closely at one of the Hubearian skeletons and he noticed puncture marks in the bones. He studied for a brief time the marks and then it hit him. These marks were the marks left by a Dioxum.

At the same time he made his discovery, we heard rumblings coming from the trees around us. Valcor looked at all of us and yelled, "Dioxum! Run!" All the creatures in our group began scattering. Instantly I saw what looked like giant spider webs being shot at all of us from the trees and rocks around us. It was complete chaos around me. I did not have the time to ask what a Dioxum was. All I had time to do was to firmly grab my staff in both my hands and hope I could make it out of the encircled area alive.

I witnessed several of our guys getting snatched by the shooting webs and being yanked into the trees around us. Everything was happening so fast. Out of the corner of my eye I saw a web shooting at me. I ducked under the web and watched it just miss me as it shot over me.

Then I heard, "Abigail! Help!" I rolled to my left and witnessed Valcor wrapped in a web. I got up and ran to help him. I used my staff to break the webbing from Valcor. He grabbed me and pulled me to the ground. "Let's crawl out of here," he said. "If we stay low they might not see us." I followed Valcor as we slowly crawled our way out of the area of the shooting webs.

Instantly it became silent. We stopped moving to look around us. Nothing was happening. As we were on our hands and knees, a large and hairy creature jumped and landed right in front of us. I was looking down towards the ground so I saw the legs of the creature. I was afraid to look up at the rest of it because its legs were scary in themselves.

As I panned my head up, I gazed upon one of the most hideous and ferocious looking creatures I had ever seen. This creature stood on two legs but had three arms on each side of its body. Its body was black and hairy. The face and head of the creature were terrifying. There were six eyes and its mouth was full of fangs. All over the face was antenna looking objects. I noticed that this creature had a long tail with what looked like a horn attached to it.

Both Valcor and I slowly stood. Valcor whispered to me, "Be still. Don't make any sudden moves. This is a Dioxum. They are deadly beasts. They are like a combination of what you would call a spider and scorpion.

Suddenly, the Dioxum reached with its six arms and grabbed me tightly. Valcor leaped at the Dioxum to try to stop it, but the Dioxum simply shot webbing from one of its hands, pinning Valcor to the ground. He could not even move.

The Dioxum raised me off the ground until it was holding me above it. Then it slowly began spinning me in circles and shooting its webbing on me at the same time. It was attempting to wrap me in a cocoon. Slowly the webbing began to cover my body. Then the webbing began to cover my head. I was beginning to have a hard time breathing. Then I became completely covered until I looked like a fly that had been wrapped by a spider in its web.

After being completely wrapped in the webbing, I heard a whistling sound go by me. The next thing I new I fell to the ground and I heard a large thud-like sound right after I hit the ground. I could hear Valcor call out to Tabukoo for help. I could not see anything but I knew something was happening around me. Then I felt someone ripping the webbing off me. As the webbing was pulled apart, I saw Tabukoo's smiling face. Tabukoo said, "There you are. Are you okay?" I told him I was okay, and he finished freeing me from the webbing.

After I was able to look around me again, I saw the Dioxum lying on the ground next to me. Tabukoo told me he shot the Dioxum in the back with an arrow which dropped it to the ground. Valcor then told the both of us that we needed to get out of the area we were in because it was a den for many Dioxum. Valcor felt like if there was one there were probably several.

Before we knew it we were surrounded by eight Dioxum. None of these Dioxum was as large as the one Tabukoo killed, but there were still eight of them surrounding us three. One of the Dioxum stepped forward and began speaking to us. It said, "You have killed our den mother. Now prepare to die for what you have done."

Instantaneously all eight of the Dioxum charged us. As they charged, Valcor warned Tabukoo and me to watch out for their tails. Valcor went on to tell us that a sting from their tails meant instant death.

I took my staff and held it in a defensive position to prepare for the Dioxum to strike. The first strike came from the tail of a Dioxum. The tail came swooping around me and wrapped around my waist. I had no idea how long or strong the Dioxum's tails were.

With the Dioxum's tail wrapped around me, the Dioxum attempted to stab me in my chest with the stinger. Fortunately I had my hands free and was able to use my staff to block the sting attempt. Then I instinctively used one end of my staff to strike the Dioxum in its face. This seemed to stun the Dioxum enough to loosen its grip on me. While the Dioxum was distracted, I freed myself from its tail, grabbed the stinger at the end of its tail, and drove the stinger into the Dioxum's body. The Dioxum immediately fell to the ground.

The other Dioxum saw what had happened. They all began shooting their webbing at us. I yelled to Valcor and Tabukoo to duck to the ground. We all three did this, causing the webbing from the remaining seven Dioxum to stick together above us. Then I took my staff and run it through the middle of the webbing.

I told Tabukoo to grab my ankles and begin swinging me in a circular motion. So he did. As Tabukoo swung me in a circle, the webbing which was attached to my staff pulled the seven Dioxum off the ground. In an instant all of the Dioxum were going in a circle. I yelled at Tabukoo to continue swinging us until the webbing flew off my staff and sent the Dioxum away from us.

It didn't take long. The force from Tabukoo swinging us caused the webbing to slide up my staff until it reached the end. Then off flew the webbing and off flew the Dioxum. They flew right out of sight. Tabukoo then gently brought me to a stop and allowed me to regain my senses. Then all three of us quickly left the area.

Our immediate concern was escaping the Dioxum. Our next concern was finding the rest of our group. It seemed that they had all disappeared, including the unicorn. It was strange to me how all of them could just disappear like they did, especially the unicorn. But there was not a single trace of evidence that any of them were in the area. We felt like we had left the den of the Dioxum and entered a ghost town. Not a sign of life anywhere.

The reason could be that we escaped the den of the Dioxum on a different side than the others. We actually came out of the den on the opposite side from which we entered. This meant we could continue in the right direction. The others may have retreated to the direction from which we all came, putting them on the opposite side of the den of the Dioxum.

Needless to say, at this point it looked like it was just us three remaining. Our hope was that the others would catch up eventually but we could not wait around for that uncertainty to happen. So we pressed onward towards the camp of Rapator.

The Ambush

Valcor, Tabukoo, and I continued on our journey until late that night. We kept going until we just could not make it any further without resting. All three of us decided to lie down on the ground to grab some quick sleep.

Early the next morning, while the dew was still wet on the ground and the fog was still heavy, we had our sleep disturbed by a ruckus from the woods. Because of all that we had just been through, our alert level was on high.

We quickly got up and began surveying the woods around us. It was eerily quiet. There was not a sound coming from the woods. No insect noise could be heard. No bird noises could be heard. Absolutely nothing could be heard.

The three of us stood with our backs against each other, looking in the woods, embracing ourselves for another attack from an unknown enemy. From the woods came creatures of all different sizes and kinds. The one common factor about all of them was that they wore what looked like black and red clothing. Each of the creatures held a staff in their hands. As they stood around us, I counted a total number of fifteen.

Valcor described the creatures as the Wardorfs. He went on further to explain that the Wardorfs were considered the elite fighting warriors of the evil horde in which Rapator led. Valcor then said, "It is an ambush. Get ready."

Tabukoo, while looking at all the creatures around us, said, "What's that human saying you use, 'Just another day at the office'?"

I nervously responded, "Yes, Tabukoo, that's right. It's just another day at the office."

Then the creatures came at us. Valcor and I had our staffs. Tabukoo, of course, had his size and strength. Five of the creatures came at me at once. My first response was to meet them and not wait on them to get to me. I gripped one end of my staff and swung in a circular movement, stopping the creatures in their tracks.

Each of the five creatures in front of me began attacking me with their staffs, driving me backwards a few steps. I was able to block their attacks and separate the creatures. This turned out to be a big disadvantage to me because now they had me surrounded instead of being able to keep all of them in sights at once.

One of the Wardorfs struck me in my lower back with his staff, sending me to the ground. As I kneeled on one knee, all five of them came at me with their staffs. As they came within striking distance of my staff, I was able to connect a blow to their knees by swinging my staff. A couple of them went to the ground while the others backed away from me.

At that moment I was able to regain my stance and prepare for the second wave of attacks from the Wardorfs. For a brief instance I was able to view Valcor and Tabukoo as they engaged their share of the Wardorfs. It was evident that they were in the fight of their lives also.

Instantly one of the Wardorfs came at me swinging his staff in an offensive manner which I had not seen. My staff said to me, "Abigail, be brave." I then moved to engage the Wardorf. Suddenly my staff began moving in ways that I did not know it could. I was fending off the moves of the Wardorf and didn't even know how I was doing it.

A second Wardorf then came at me from my right side. I was now in battle with two Wardorfs. This Wardorf was swinging for my head. As I fought off the swings of the first Wardorf, I had to duck and dodge the swings of the second.

As I was defending myself from the two Wardorfs, I heard from behind me a loud "thud" sound. Right after that sound I was hit from behind by Tabukoo. The impact from Tabukoo sent me twenty feet on the ground from where I was fighting. Fortunately I stopped before I hit any rocks or trees around us.

Slightly dazed, I was able to get to my feet and witness several of the Wardorfs using their staffs to beat Tabukoo relentlessly. Every blow took one more breath out of Tabukoo's life. I knew I had to get to him to help him before the Wardorfs beat him to death. At the time I did not realize that I was bleeding from my head and leg. When I attempted to step towards Tabukoo, I became dizzy and lost my balance. It was then that I realized that

I was bleeding. The jolt from Tabukoo's impact must have caused more trauma to my body than I realized.

I could only watch helplessly as the Wardorfs continued their onslaught on Tabukoo. Finally, Tabukoo stopped moving. I thought the Wardorfs had killed Tabukoo so I screamed, "Tabukoo! No!" Three of the Wardorfs who were beating Tabukoo looked at me and then headed in my direction.

I knew I had to find a way to regain my composure and defend myself. If I could not, the approaching Wardorfs were going to treat me the same as they did Tabukoo. As the three Wardorfs came closer, I noticed that the remaining Wardorfs drug Tabukoo's body out of sight and into the surrounding trees from which they came from. It was a strange sight and for a brief moment it confused me as to why they would do such a thing. However, I did not have the time to figure it out as the approaching Wardorfs were coming close.

Somehow I was able to get to my feet just in time to defend myself. As soon as I stood, the Wardorfs went on the attack again. The force from all three of the Wardorfs hitting me sent me back against a large rock behind me. The impact of hitting the rock caused me to lose my grip around my staff.

All three Wardorfs leaped at me. As they were in the air, I was able to grab my staff. The Wardorfs landed in front of me and drove their staffs towards my chest. I used my staff to block their attack, sending their staffs upwards. While the Wardorfs had their arms outstretched, I quickly jabbed all three of them in their stomachs, sending them backwards.

That was all the space I needed to move from the rock so I wouldn't be trapped in a corner. I drove the end of my staff into the ground and flipped myself over the three Wardorfs, landing behind them. As they turned to face me, I swung my staff at them, striking them across their faces. All three fell backwards and hit the ground.

Next, I turned to check on Valcor. He was engaged with seven of the Wardorfs. I attempted to run to him to help, but was cut off by five more Wardorfs, each eager to take me on. Still physically weak but mentally confident, I prepared for a fight.

Remembering my training from my early childhood as a gymnast, I did cartwheels in the direction of the five Wardorfs standing between Valcor and me. Then I stopped right in front of them, doing a handstand. While suspended upside down, I could tell the Wardorfs were confused. So I took advantage of that moment and surprised them by twisting my lower body in a way that sent my feet kicking straight into their faces.

Each Wardorf went backwards, a couple of them even falling to the ground. Then I grabbed my staff, threw it in the air, and jumped off the back of one of the fallen Wardorfs. I grabbed my staff in mid air and used it to strike three of the Wardorfs, sending them to the ground. At that point all five were lying on the ground.

One of the Wardorfs on the ground close to me kicked dirt into my eyes, temporarily blinding me. Now they had the advantage over me. Without warning I felt blows from their staffs hit me on the backside of my left leg, right above the back of my knee. Instantly I was knocked to the ground as the blows knocked my legs out from under me.

In that moment, I could hear my staff, which I still held in my hands, begin to speak to me. My staff said, "Abigail, listen to me. I will be your eyes." I really did not have much a choice as I lay there on the ground at the complete mercy of my enemy.

My staff then said, "Roll to your right." So I did what I was told, just barely moving out of the way of a staff thrust from one of the Wardorfs. "Now, jump to your feet," my staff said. I immediately got up and held my staff close to my ears so I could hear my staff's voice.

My staff then told me to jump and bend my legs at my knees. One of the Wardorfs used his staff to make a swipe at my ankles. I narrowly missed the staff as it went under me. My staff then said, "Now quickly jab me straight ahead of you as far as you can reach." I trusted my staff's wisdom and did as it instructed. I could feel an impact as I struck one of the Wardorfs in the nose, sending the creature to the ground in a pool of blood.

The other Wardorfs around me stood in amazement that I could inflict such a wound while not being able to see. My staff instructed me to turn and swing the staff as hard as I could while the other Wardorfs stood in shock. When I did I felt the vibrations run through my arms as I connected my staff with something large.

In a split second I heard something turn over and was knocked to the ground by what I could only imagine in my mind to be a large wave of water. Apparently my staff was familiar with our surroundings and knew that right above me was a large body of water contained in a basin created by dead trees trapped in a mass of rocks. My staff told me to hit the front of a rock that supported all the water above us. By doing so I dislodged the rock and caused the water to spill downwards, washing all of us away.

After the water subsided and I was able to regain my strength, I opened my eyes and found that I could see again. Apparently, the rush of the water washed out the dirt in my eyes. I looked around me and saw Valcor, along with many Wardorfs, lying on the ground.

I rushed to Valcor while I had the chance. He was lying on the ground. Rolling him over, I noticed he was conscious and breathing. He looked at me and told me I did a great job. I asked Valcor if he was alright. He said he thought he was, other than being sore from all the fighting.

I held Valcor in my arms while he rested on the ground. As I did, the Wardorfs all gathered around us. I told Valcor that it looked like we were not done fighting as we had become surrounded. Valcor told me that the Wardorfs will not give up. They will continue until either we are dead or they are dead.

I gently lowered Valcor's head to the ground and told him, "Then I guess my work isn't done yet." After I laid Valcor's head on the ground, I slowly and unknowingly to the Wardorfs grasped my staff in my left hand. I jumped to feet in a flash and said, "Okay, all you creatures. If it's a fight you want, then it's a fight you'll get." I just stood there in a battle stance ready for whatever the Wardorfs would bring my way.

Then a voice from behind the Wardorfs shouted, "Enough! Lower your staffs my warriors." Each of the Wardorfs lowered their staffs. Then a couple of them parted to reveal Rapator. My heart beat with anger and frustration as my eyes beheld him.

Rapator then approached Valcor and me. He stopped just outside of my staff's striking range. Rapator then said, "So, human, we meet again. Although this time it looks like I have the advantage."

I responded, "Why don't you come a little closer and we will find out who has the advantage?"

Rapator smirked and said, "So you can attempt to hit me with your staff?" Rapator was many things but stupid was not one of them.

I asked if he was afraid to give me the chance.

His response was, "In due time human…in due time. We have other things to discuss right now." I asked Rapator what he was talking about. Rapator said, "I am talking about the future of your best friend. Would you like to know how Chelsea is doing?"

I replied, "You better not have harmed her. If you have I will make you pay for it!"

"Easy now," Rapator said. "Why do you think I would harm her? On the contrary, I have taken good care of your friend. I would like you to see her again. So I am making you an offer."

"What kind of offer?" I half-heartedly asked of him.

Rapator then said, "I would like to escort you and Valcor to my camp where you can meet her and even talk to her. What do you think about that?"

I then said, "I don't know if I can trust any escort you could give. How do I know you are not trying to set some trap for us?"

Rapator responded, "You don't know if I'm setting a trap or not. But if you want to see and speak to your friend again, you need to take that chance. If you don't take my offer now, not only will you never see Chelsea again but you, along with Valcor, will not live to see tomorrow. The only thing standing in the way of my Wardorfs finishing the both of you right now is my order to stand down. I can easily give them the order to finish the both of you. It makes no difference to me."

"If it makes no difference to you, then why would you allow me to have the opportunity to see Chelsea? Why wouldn't you just go ahead and destroy me now?" I asked.

Rapator said, "Believe me, I would love nothing more than to take care of you at this moment. However, Chelsea made a request that I spare you, at least for now. She would like to see you."

"Why would you listen to the request of Chelsea? Why would you show such compassion on your prisoner?" I asked. Rapator then told me that his plans have changed due to unexpected circumstances.

So I looked at Valcor and thought about Rapator's option of seeing Chelsea. We were heading to rescue Chelsea anyway, so perhaps it would be easier this way as opposed to fighting. So I turned to Rapator and said, "Let's do it."

I helped Valcor to his feet. The Wardorfs surrounded the both of us and led us behind Rapator. As they escorted us to Rapator's camp, I became anxious to see Chelsea again but fearful of what may have become of her. Either way, I was about to find out.

The Meeting

We finally arrived at Rapator's camp. As we entered his camp I noticed a wide variety of creatures that had joined his evil crusade. Many of the creatures I had never seen before. Some of them were hideous but surprisingly most were not. Every creature stopped what they were doing as we walked by them. One thing they all had in common was their look of hatred towards me. Each one looked at me with an evil look in their eyes.

Rapator escorted Valcor and me to an open space located within his camp. There Rapator ordered the Wardorfs to leave us. Now it was just the three of us together. Rapator looked at Valcor and me and told us to wait here. Soon we would be able to see and speak with Chelsea.

Minutes later, one of the Wardorfs arrived and told Rapator that the human girl was ready. At that moment, Rapator had the Wardorf lead Valcor out of the area, leaving Rapator and me alone. Once alone, Rapator said to me, "Well, little girl, mighty chosen one, here is your chance to see your friend again. But let me warn you about something. Prepare yourself for what you are about to see because this may be the last time you get to see her." Then Rapator walked away.

After Rapator left my sight, I heard a ruffling sound coming from the brush where he exited. To my excitement Chelsea came from the brush. I saw her and ran to her. Chelsea ran to me and we both embraced one another. We were both so happy to see each other again that we did not say anything momentarily. We just hugged and laughed.

Finally I was able to say to her, "Chelsea! I have missed you so much and have so worried about you. How are you? Has Rapator mistreated you or hurt you in any way?"

Chelsea smiled and answered, "Abigail, slow down. I'm good. Rapator did make it hard on me for a while."

I looked at her body and saw wounds on her arms and ankles. My joy quickly turned to sadness and then anger. I said to Chelsea, "I see those marks on your body! What has he done to you to cause those marks? I am going to…"

Chelsea interrupted me at that point and said to me, "Abigail, listen to me. It is alright. Rapator's abuse has stopped. He did make my life miserable in the beginning of my capture but has since changed his treatment of me. In fact, recently Rapator has treated me with respect and like royalty. He has offered me the best of food, lodging, and even threatened all the evil creatures in his camp to do no harm to me unless they want to be put to death."

"Wait a minute, Chelsea," I said to her. "You mean to tell me that Rapator has actually treated you decently?"

Chelsea responded, "Yes he has."

I then said, "There has to be a reason why. Why do you think he has shown a sudden change in attitude?"

Chelsea then took a couple of steps away from me. She then began walking around the area in which we were located. Chelsea then asked me, "Do you remember when we were ten and we got into a really big fight over my little cousin?"

I answered, "Yeah. We almost threw away our friendship that day. I think we were the closest that day than any other time of walking out of each other's life."

Chelsea then said, "That was a terrible day for us. I'm glad we chose to but our differences behind us instead of ending our friendship."

I then commented, "I don't even remember why we had that argument over your little cousin, do you?"

Chelsea then answered, "Yes, I do." Chelsea then stopped walking and looked at me. She then said, "My little cousin had fed your cat a piece of chocolate, not knowing that your cat was allergic to chocolate."

I then added, "Oh yeah! Now I remember. My cat almost died. I got really mad at your little cousin for doing that."

"Yes you did, Abigail," Chelsea said. "In fact, you were so angry that not only did you refuse to forgive my little cousin, but you grew angry with me. You tried to blame me because my little cousin was in my family. Because of that anger, we almost split up."

I responded, "Yeah, I was a big butt hole. I am so glad that I forgave your little cousin and wised up about it not being your fault. I don't know how I could have lived without you being my best friend."

Chelsea said to me, "I'm glad you forgave my little cousin also. Abigail, you have been my best friend for a long time now. I think we have a special relationship, don't you?"

I answered, "Yes."

Chelsea then told me, "I once again have a favor to ask you. I need you to forgive my family once again."

I asked, "What do you mean Chelsea?"

Chelsea continued, "Well, you know how your great grandfather arrived here in the land of the Crystal Sea with another man? And it turned out that your great grandfather and that man were friends? And that your great grandfather and his friend disagreed about what to do to fix the problems they created in this land?"

I said to Chelsea, "What are you trying to tell me? Of course I remember all of that stuff."

Chelsea then continued, "Your great grandfather loved his friend enough that he could not kill his friend so he had his friend imprisoned in a ball of ice."

I looked in Chelsea's eyes and asked her, "What are you trying to say to me, Chelsea? Just get at your point."

Chelsea then said, "Your great grandfather's friend was actually…my great grandfather." We both just stared at each other for a brief moment as the meaning of that realization ran through our brains.

Chelsea then said, "Abigail, you are my best friend. We are best friends just like our great grandfathers. But I do not want our friendship to end like their relationship did."

I quickly blurted, "Neither do I, Chelsea. We still have that choice. Our destiny is in our hands to keep that from happening."

Chelsea then responded, "But Abigail, you want to kill my great grandfather."

Realizing where we were headed in our conversation, I turned my back to Chelsea and took a few steps. Then I said with my back to her, "Yes, Chelsea, I do. But you know as well as I do that it has to be done in order to restore this land to its original state."

There was silence in the air. Then I turned to look at Chelsea and asked her, "Now that you know the beast is your great grandfather, does that fact change your opinion about what needs to be done?"

Chelsea then said, "Actually it does. Abigail, I know the beast is the beast for a reason. My great grandfather created havoc in this land and has done a lot of evil here. But despite all that I can't change the fact he is still my great grandfather. He is still part of my family. I guess, I am also part of him."

I said to her, "Chelsea, you are not part of the beast. Whatever the beast is now, it can't be what your great grandfather was before he became the beast. The beast is completely evil and destructive. You know that."

Chelsea said back to me, "I understand all that, Abigail. I was hoping that maybe you could do the same thing you did with my little cousin and forgive my great grandfather for his actions."

"I wish it was that simple, Chelsea. I would love nothing more than to be able to forgive the beast and all of the

Crystal Sea would become better. I don't want to have to kill the beast. I don't want to have to fight each day I am in this land just to survive. However, I don't think either you or I have much of a choice. You know the prophecies just like I do."

With sorrow in her eyes, Chelsea said to me, "I know the prophecies but who's to say we can't change those prophecies? Why can't we just leave this land? Or why can't we free the beast and talk to my great grandfather? Maybe when he realized who I was he would listen to me and come to his senses."

"The beast is not able to reasonably discuss things, Chelsea. Now that your great grandfather has turned to the beast, we have no way of freeing him other than by killing him. Only then will your great grandfather become your great grandfather again," I said to Chelsea.

"There has got to be a different way of handling things other than killing my great grandfather! Come on, Abigail, think! There has got to be a better way," Chelsea begged me.

Seeing tears in Chelsea's eyes, I walked over to her and grasped her upper arms in my hands. I softly said to her, "Chelsea, there is no other way. We must remain focused. I know the beast is your great grandfather, but we have got to put all things behind us and fulfill our purpose."

Then Chelsea spread her arms out and knocked my hands off her. She took a few steps around me, walking behind me. Then she said, "That's easy for you to say, Abigail. We are not talking about killing your great grandfather. No, in fact, your great grandfather was the great hero of this land. You are just following in his footsteps. But my great grandfather was the great villain and I am faced with the decision of following in his footsteps."

I turned to Chelsea and said, "Chelsea, you don't have to follow the beast's footsteps. You can choose to be good and resist the evil that is tempting you right now."

Chelsea began raising her voice at me when she said, "And that is another thing. Stop calling my great grandfather the 'beast'. He is still my family. He is still my great grandfather and I cannot believe after meeting with you like this that you would even consider killing a member of my family!"

I thought for a moment and then asked, "What do you mean 'after meeting with me?' Did Rapator set up this time with you for your benefit? Were you hoping to speak with me in hopes of using our friendship to change my mind about killing the beast?"

Chelsea then said, "It sounds a little bad the way you ask those questions. I love you, Abigail. My intent of meeting with you today was to see you again. I guess in my heart I had hoped I could also get you to change your mind about killing my great grandfather. I guess there's no way you will do that, huh?"

"You are right, Chelsea. I can't change my mind. To change my mind would be to give up on my purpose. To change my mind would also be giving up on this land's creatures' hope for restoration," I said to her.

Chelsea responded, "Your attitude is very disturbing to me, Abigail. I thought we were best friends. But I guess I was wrong."

I said to Chelsea, "We are best friends. How could you deny that?"

Chelsea walked towards me and said, "Best friends don't kill each other's family." As Chelsea looked at me, I could see her eyes begin to change colors. Here pupils changed to a corn yellow. She then went on to say, "Abigail, if you will not change your mind about killing my great grandfather, then consider our friendship over."

I said, "What are you saying, Chelsea? Don't do this. I don't know what Rapator has been telling you but don't believe him."

Chelsea interrupted me and said, "It appears that Rapator is the only one I can trust around here. The things he told me have come true. He told me that the beast is my great grandfather. He told me that it would do me no good to attempt to change your mind. He said you would react the exact way that you have. Rapator told me you would deny our friendship and choose to continue on your journey to find my great grandfather and kill him."

At this point I did not know how to respond or what to expect. Inside I felt like part of me was being ripped out. Chelsea had been such a needed part of my life for so long and now we were being torn apart.

Suddenly Rapator entered where Chelsea and I were standing. I looked at him and angrily asked, "What are you doing here?" Rapator told me it was time for Chelsea to leave. I was so angry with Rapator. He had brainwashed my best friend in to becoming my enemy. I wasn't about to let him get away with it.

I rushed Rapator in hopes of getting him to the ground. If I could do that I wasn't sure what I would do next. I leaped at Rapator but he was able to block my kick and knock me backwards to the ground. I laid there on my back as Rapator said, "Pathetic you are the so called chosen one. Do you really think that you could defeat me if we fought? I would dispose of you in a hurry."

While I lay there, Chelsea looked at me with a combination of sorrow and anger. I knew that things were changing quickly. My best friend in my whole life was about to leave me and join forces with Rapator. I could not believe that all of this was happening.

Rapator then told us that he would allow Chelsea to say her goodbyes to me before he escorted her away from me. I rose to my feet and dusted off the dirt from my clothes.

Chelsea looked at me and said, "I guess there is not much to say anymore. You have chosen your path and I have chosen mine. Your path has you taking a life and my path has me preserving a life. You tell me who the hero and the villain are. I still can't believe you would kill my great grandfather."

I told Chelsea, "Sometimes doing the right thing is the hardest thing to choose to do. In fact, the easiest thing to do is usually the wrong thing. You say that you choose to preserve life. Do you understand that the one you want to preserve is the one who is the author of all the evil in this land?"

Chelsea said to me, "The only thing I understand is that I want my great grandfather to live. If that means stopping you from killing him, then that is what I will have to do."

Then Chelsea's skin began to change in color and appearance. She then warned me, "Abigail, don't cross my path again!"

Chelsea told Rapator she was ready to leave. Rapator called some Wardorfs to stand guard around me and the two of them left my sight. As Chelsea walked away, I just broke down in sorrow, burying my face in my chest.

The Betrayal

As Chelsea was escorted away from me by Rapator, her eyes filled with tears as she knew deep in her soul that she had just crossed a boundary with me that was almost impossible to cross back. Chelsea realized that she had just chosen sides in this conflict and it was not the side she thought was the good side. However, she was willing to risk what was good, to even risk her relationship with me, her best friend, in order to stay loyal to her family.

I stood surrounded by Wardorfs, all alone. I just witnessed my best friend betray me, and what was right. I never thought that Chelsea and I would ever reach that point. It was then that I accepted the fact that to follow my purpose would cost me dearly and I had to be willing to sacrifice everything to fulfill that purpose.

Not only was I without my best friend, but also I was without Valcor and Tabukoo. I had no idea where either of them was. So in my point of isolation I began thinking about what the Creator had made this land like in the beginning. It wasn't the Creator's intent for all this evil to create chaos in this once marvelous land. The evil and chaos around me was a direct result of my family's and Chelsea's family's influence.

The land's cries for help just got louder and louder as I stood there. I was the only one who could hear those cries. The Wardorfs couldn't hear them. Only I could. The urgency to fulfill my purpose grew stronger and stronger. I had a deep conviction that now, more than ever, I had to remain faithful and trust the Creator that He knew what he was doing in giving me this mission.

There was no time to feel sorry for myself. The life of this land and the life of my best friend, as well as my own life, all were at stake. It was time to take charge of my situation. I did not know where Valcor or Tabukoo were but I wasn't about to stand around and let them down.

With the Wardorfs standing around me and me not having my staff, I had to think of a way to get out from the Wardorfs, find my friends, find my staff, and get us back on our path to finding the beast.

While standing under the guard of the Wardorfs, I heard a noise from the sky. I looked up and I saw the unicorn. The unicorn swept down to where I was. As the Wardorfs came at us, the unicorn kicked them backwards. I quickly hopped on the unicorn's back and he flew us into the sky.

I told the unicorn that we had to find Valcor and Tabukoo. The unicorn then asked about Chelsea and I let the unicorn know that Chelsea had chosen where she belonged.

With hearing about Chelsea, the unicorn began flying us in circles high above Rapator's camp. We slowly descended to where we could get a better view of the camp, hoping to spot Valcor and Tabukoo.

Without warning, a large rock went flying by us. Before we could react, another rock flew past us on the other side. We were being shot at by Rapator's army below us. They were using catapults to fire their large rocks at us, hoping to knock us out of the sky.

The unicorn was doing what he could to dodge the large rocks. Sometimes he would move so suddenly that I would have to cling to the unicorn with all my strength to keep from falling off.

Then I was able to spot Tabukoo and Valcor. They were being held captive together in an open spot in the woods near the side of a mountain. I showed the unicorn where they were and instructed him to fly us near the spot.

As the unicorn headed for a nearby place to land, one of the large rocks hit the unicorn in his back legs. Then we began falling to the ground. The unicorn told me to hold on and prepare for a hard landing. He did the best he could to lessen our impact when we hit the ground but we still hit extremely hard, sending me off the unicorn's back and into a pile of brush.

For a brief moment I lost consciousness. When I awoke I could hear many creatures talking off in a distance. I slowly opened my eyes and looked straight ahead. I could see several creatures surrounding the unicorn. It looked like the unicorn might have died in the impact but I could not tell.

Apparently the creatures had not noticed me lying in the brush. So I just lay there quietly and very still, while watching the creatures standing around the unicorn. My heart broke for the unicorn. He had been such a loyal friend. He ultimately gave his life for the cause of restoring this land to its original condition.

I wish I could have done something for the unicorn but I knew I could not do anything. The only thing I could do was make sure the creatures did not capture me. Valcor and Tabukoo both needed me to rescue them.

While the creatures were focused on the unicorn, I quietly slipped away into the woods. I was able to hide from many creatures running through the woods. Sometimes I would hide behind a tree. Sometimes I had to duck behind a rock. I hid each time a creature headed my way.

After a while I was able to make my way to where Valcor and Tabukoo were being held. While I surveyed the area, I was able to spot my staff. It was leaning against a tree trunk on the opposite side of the opening. So I slowly made my way to where the staff was.

I examined the situation as I made my way for my staff. Valcor and Tabukoo were being guarded by twelve Wardorfs and several creatures which I had not seen before. It was going to take a miracle for little me to free my friends but I had to give it a shot.

Finally I was able to reach the tree in which my staff rested on. Slowly I reached around the tree. With no one looking I grasped my staff and slowly moved it around the tree until I had it safely on the other side. My staff saw me and said, "Abigail! I thought I might not see you again. How did you find me?" I tried my best to quiet my staff down as I knew it was speaking loud enough for the creatures guarding Valcor and Tabukoo to hear.

My staff apologized for its loudness and promised to keep quiet. But unfortunately it was too late, we had been discovered. I could hear one of the creatures yell, "Who's there? The staff, it's gone. Check it out." Two creatures went around each side of the tree in which the staff used to be resting on. When they made it to the backside of the tree they found nothing.

One of the creatures reported there was no one there and returned to guard Valcor and Tabukoo. Thankfully they did not notice I was up in the tree, right above where they were standing. At least this time, I dodged a big bullet.

I was able to climb down the tree and head for some bushes at the base of a tree closer to Valcor and Tabukoo. Once I made it to the bushes, I hid there and tried to formulate a plan to get Valcor and Tabukoo out of there.

While hiding in the bushes, Rapator and Chelsea appeared in the clearing. Rapator began explaining to the Wardorfs and other creatures that the unicorn had been shot from the sky but they did not find me. So Rapator warned the guards to be on the look out for me.

Rapator was then told of my staff disappearing. Rapator then told them to be ready because my staff disappearing could only mean one thing…that I was close and I was going to attempt to free Valcor and Tabukoo.

From the bushes I noticed Valcor and Tabukoo looking in the woods to see if they could see me. At the same time I noticed Chelsea scanning the woods as well. I still could not get used to the fact that my best friend was against me now.

For no reason, Rapator walked over to the bushes where I was hiding. He turned his back to me and continued to warn the creatures to be on guard. I thought that I had an advantage with Rapator not facing me. In my mind I formulated a plan of trade. I would grab Rapator from behind and hold him as trade bait to free my friends.

So I went for it. I sprung from the bushes and drove my staff right into the base of Rapator's spine. The pressure from my staff caused Rapator to fall to his knees and down to the ground. I then stood above him with my staff directly on his spine, pinning Rapator motionless.

All the creatures made movements to come at me but I warned them to stop or I would permanently injure Rapator. Rapator then gave the order for all the creatures to remain still. Then he said to me, "I wondered how long it would take for you to find your friends."

I responded to Rapator by saying, "Now you have your answer. What I want is for you to free Valcor and Tabukoo. Then I want you to allow us to leave your camp without being pursued."

Rapator answered back, "You are asking a lot little girl. You presume much as well." Then after I drove my staff a little deeper in his spine, Rapator said, "Okay! Okay! I get your point." Rapator then ordered the release of Valcor and Tabukoo.

As Valcor and Tabukoo were being released, I looked at Chelsea and asked her, "Chelsea, will you come with us?"

Chelsea replied, "To kill my great grandfather? I don't think so." Then Chelsea looked at me with an anger I had never seen within her before. She looked as if she wanted to inflict harm on me.

Rapator then said, "I hope you realize you are not going to accomplish your purpose. We will stop you. Chelsea will stop you." I just looked at Chelsea the whole time Rapator spoke. I could see the hate and bitterness within Chelsea grow right before me.

Chelsea's appearance slowly began changing as her hate and bitterness grew. Her hair grew longer and not just on her head. Her hair grew longer all over her body. Her eyes began turning completely yellow in color. She looked taller as well. Chelsea's surrender to evil was transforming her just like it did her great grandfather. Chelsea was becoming another beast.

I warned Chelsea, "Look at you, Chelsea. You are changing into a beast, just like your great grandfather did. Is that what you want?" Chelsea then started looking at herself. She raised her hands and looked hard at them, examining the change. Then she gently touched her face, feeling the hair along her cheek.

Chelsea then looked at me with a look in her eyes that said, "Abigail, I am so sorry." I said to Chelsea, "It's not too late, Chelsea. You can decide to forsake Rapator, the beast, and all they stand for."

Then Chelsea responded, "It's too late for me, Abigail. I'm sorry for what I am about to do." I was not too sure what she meant by that statement but I would find out soon enough.

I watched as Chelsea reached in a pocket on her pants. She pulled out a device that I had no clue what it was. It was shaped similarly to a boomerang but sleeker and longer. Chelsea threw the device above her in the air. It took off at an incredible speed until it went out of sight.

Then I placed my attention back on Chelsea. She had an evil grin come across her face. Out of nowhere I heard a whistle sound. It was the device Chelsea through in the air. The device flew in front of me, knocking my staff out of my hands.

Immediately Rapator jumped to his feet and that is when things went crazy. Wardorfs began attacking Valcor and Tabukoo. Other creatures came for me. Rapator and Chelsea just stood in the midst of the chaos and watched to see what would happen.

I noticed a tree limb right above my head. I jumped up and grabbed the limb. While hanging on the limb I kicked the creatures coming at me. That gave me a brief window of opportunity to reach my staff and prepare for a fight.

My staff went into a windmill action as the creatures approached me. As the creatures thrust their staffs at me, I was able to block their thrusts with my staff. Then I used my staff to strike each creature around me in their knee caps, sending them to the ground.

One of the Wardorfs saw that I had gained the advantage over the other creatures and made his way through all the chaos to take me on in battle. This Wardorf was not like the others. This Wardorf was the largest I had ever seen. He looked at me and introduced himself, "Hello Abigail. I was hoping we would get a chance to challenge each other's skills. I have heard much about your skills. My name is Lord Shnikel and I am the leader of all the Wardorfs."

I guess he thought that he was going to impress me with his position and size before ending my life, but honestly I wasn't too impressed. I said back to him, "Lord Shnikel. Your name sounds like a sandwich." He did not like my response and aggressively came at me.

With one swing of his staff he knocked me backwards several feet and I landed on my back. Lord Shnikel laughed and told me I was nothing but a useless, little girl who had no business thinking I could make a difference in his land. While on my back, the leader of all the Wardorfs leaped at me, landing at my feet.

The ground around me shook from his weight impacting the ground. He raised his leg and attempted to step on my chest. I held my staff in a horizontal position to block Lord Shnikel's large foot from collapsing my chest.

The power of his step was more than I had ever experienced. I could tell that Lord Shnikel's strength rivaled that of Tabukoo's. At this point I could only hope that my staff would hold up under the pressure of his stomp. Slowly Shnikel's foot got closer and closer to my chest. I knew that I was in deep trouble.

Out of the corner of my eye I could see Rapator's smirk as he was hoping I would be done in by Lord Shnikel. Rapator's smirk was all I needed to become motivated not to allow Rapator to win.

To my right, on the ground, I noticed the device Chelsea used to knock my staff out of my hands. With my right hand I was able to grab the device and drive it right through the ankle of Lord Shnikel. He immediately let up his pressure on me and fell to ground, screaming in pain. That move may have saved me for the moment, but it also made Lord Shnikel even more determined to finish me.

Lord Shnikel pulled the device out of his ankle and discarded it. As he hobbled towards me, I used my staff to engage him. We went back and forth in our conflict. Lord Shnikel was definitely a great warrior. He was much more advanced in his skill of staffing than the other Wardorfs I had fought.

As we struggled to gain advantage over each other, I noticed that Lord Shnikel was growing weaker. Part of the reason was his ankle. He had to use more energy than normal because of his injury. Once I noticed his weakness, I knew I could take advantage of him and gain the victory.

When my opportunity came in our fight, I used my staff to strike Lord Shnikel in his hurt ankle. He had no choice but to fall to the ground in agony. I then used my staff to strike him across his chin, knocking him unconscious.

Finished with Lord Shnikel, I went to assist Valcor and Tabukoo. Both were overwhelmed with the battle. I jumped in the pile of fighters. We all three could sense the momentum of the fight turning our way. Apparently, so did Rapator.

At his command, he told the Wardorfs and other creatures to stop fighting us. This was a bizarre move to us. Rapator was up to something. All the creatures moved in a circle around us. Rapator then said to us, "Enough of this petty fighting. It's obvious that you, Abigail, have skills that none of my evil creatures can match. But let's see how you match against my skill."

I stepped forward and said, "Gladly. Are you ready?"

Rapator then responded, "Oh no, Abigail. When I said my skill I meant exactly that. I have imparted all my knowledge and skill to another creature that will fight for me."

I thought to myself, *Whatever, let's do this thing.*

Then my worst nightmare came true when Rapator said, "Chelsea, you know what you have to do." Chelsea stepped forward with a staff in her hand. Although she had changed into a monster in her appearance, I knew it was still my best friend inside.

"You want me to fight Chelsea?" I asked Rapator.

"Chelsea is not Chelsea any longer. She is now a beast in training, preparing to come along side of her great grandfather. And if you, Abigail, want to accomplish your mission, you have to first go through Chelsea."

I could not bear the thought of fighting Chelsea. I shook my head in disbelief. Valcor then reminded me, "Abigail, you have to do this. I know it must be so very hard but if you don't, we perish along with all this land." Valcor's words were true but I was struggling with having to fight my best friend.

Chelsea wasted no time in showing how she felt. She charged me with her staff in the air. She was on top of me before I could react. She then struck me in my stomach, causing me to bend over. Then while I was bent over, she swung her staff upwards, hitting me in my chin. I was knocked off the ground, falling on my side.

All the evil creatures around us began cheering. They sensed Chelsea had gotten the best of me. Chelsea then struck me across my back, inflicting horrific pain throughout my body. Chelsea then shouted, "Come on, Abigail! Fight me! Get up and show me what you have!"

Tabukoo looked at me and said softly, "You can do it. Face your fears and trust in who you know you are according to the Creator's purpose." I had a hard time regaining my balance but I was able to get back on my feet. I turned to Chelsea and noticed she had changed even more. I was losing her and it was breaking my heart.

Chelsea then thrust her staff at me, striking me right between my eyes. I had to embrace my staff and use it a support to keep from falling to the ground again. Again, the creatures around us cheered.

Using her staff, Chelsea then knocked my feet out from under me. While in mid air, she grabbed me with her hands and threw me several feet across the field into a pile of rocks. At that point I lost all feeling in my body. I was bleeding really badly and felt like I was losing my life. Then Chelsea grabbed me and lifted me above her head. As I hung there above her, the creatures around us cheered even louder. They all began screaming for my destruction.

I could not bring myself to strike my best friend. All I could do was forgive her and love here unconditionally. We had been through so much as friends I just could not imagine bringing harm against her. I cherished Chelsea, even though she had transformed into a terrible monster.

While suspended above Chelsea, I turned to Valcor with a look to tell him how sorry I was that I could not bring myself to fight Chelsea. I knew I had let him down, as well as all of the land of the Crystal Sea. Tears flowed from Valcor's face as he looked back at me as if to say he understood why I couldn't fight Chelsea.

Little did any of us know that while Chelsea held me in the air above her head, there was still a little part of the human Chelsea still trying to regain her old self. Chelsea looked at all the creatures around us and listened to their chants of destruction. Strangely enough those chants struck a part of Chelsea that desired for goodness.

Instead of finishing me that instant, she dropped me to the ground. Everyone around us went silent. Chelsea stood above me and said, "Enough is enough. Killing Abigail is something I can't do. As much as I should in order to save my great grandfather, Abigail is still my friend."

Rapator stepped in and challenged Chelsea, "If you don't finish Abigail right now then you cannot sit at the side of your great grandfather."

Chelsea said back, "I cannot finish her."

Rapator angrily said, "This is unacceptable!" Then he slapped Chelsea, knocking her against a rock.

"I'll do it then," Rapator proclaimed. Rapator then picked up a rock and held it over my head. His plan was to drop it on me to crush my skull.

But Chelsea ran at Rapator and knocked him down, saving me this time at least. Chelsea then said to Rapator, "I said that Abigail does not have to die, and I will not allow you to harm her any more."

Rapator spread his wings and flew over Chelsea. As he flew above her, he grabbed Chelsea, lifting her off the ground. Once Rapator got Chelsea in the air, he flew her directly into the side of large boulder. After the impact, he dropped her and allowed her to fall to the ground.

Then Rapator flew downwards and struck Chelsea in the back of her head, knocking her unconscious. Rapator then landed next to Chelsea. He proceeded to tell all the creatures listening that he was going to make an example of Chelsea. He was going to show all the creatures what happens when someone betrays him.

I couldn't help but compare the difference between good and evil. When Chelsea betrayed me all I could do was display forgiveness and love. However, when Chelsea betrayed Rapator, he wanted to display revenge and hatred. What a difference. No doubt it was easier to take revenge and hate someone, but easy does not make it right.

Rapator then bent over Chelsea and with his powerful hands, grasped the neck of Chelsea. With every second he squeezed the life out of my best friend. I had to somehow find the strength left in me to do something to save Chelsea. That's when I saw the device Chelsea used earlier. I crawled over to it and picked it up.

That moment I felt myself beginning to pass out. I knew it was now or never. I hurled the device towards Rapator. He must have heard the device coming at him because he turned to see it coming his way. Just in time he dodged out of its way. He laughed and said, "You missed. Too bad for you, and Chelsea."

I fell to the ground and as things were going black, I was able to see the device circle around and catch Rapator in the back of his head, causing him to drop to the side.

Then things went completely black. I had passed out from exhaustion.

Later, when I regained consciousness, the first thing I saw was Chelsea in her beastly form sitting next to me. She said, "Welcome to the land of the living."

I sat up and looked around us. We were in some sort of cave. We had a fire to warm us. Then I asked, "What happened? Where are we?"

Chelsea responded, "We are in a cave within the mountain. Apparently you saved my life. I guess I should be thankful but I would have better off dead. Anyway, thank you."

I said back, "That's what friends do. They help one another."

Chelsea then said, "Yeah, about that helping one another thing. I want to give you one more chance to help me. I want you to give up your mission. That would help me out a lot."

"Chelsea, you know I can't do that. My purpose is to free this land of its evil by destroying the beast."

Chelsea then made things tempting when she said, "You know, being the beast's great granddaughter does have its perks. I can offer you great wealth in this land. I can also offer you a great position of power. You could sit third in line, behind my great grandfather and me. Nothing would be too great for you to have."

I thought about it for a moment and responded, "I would love to have a great relationship with you again, Chelsea. However, life is not about personal gain. Life is about fulfilling our own purpose given to us by the

Creator. If I decided to accept your offer, I would gain a lot of worldly things but I would be completely miserable. I would be miserable because I would not be fulfilled inside knowing I gave up, and in the process letting many people down along the way."

Chelsea then said, "Don't you think you are being a little too dramatic about this purpose thing?"

I said, "No I don't. Sometimes our purpose will lead down a far different path than that of others. But we all wind up accomplishing the same result, which is to serve others instead of ourselves."

Chelsea then said, "I had hoped you would join me but I see that you are too stubborn to do that. So you leave me no choice." Then Chelsea stood to her feet and left me alone in the cave.

After a short time alone, two Wardorfs came to escort me out of the cave. They took me to a place in the woods where all the evil creatures were gathered around a small body of water. I looked and saw Valcor and Tabukoo standing by the water's edge. Each of them had a large stone tied to their ankles.

I asked Chelsea what was going on. She said, "Thanks to your actions, Rapator is no longer with us. And because of that, I have taken charge of this army. For my first order of business, I am ordering the execution of Valcor and Tabukoo. What I am going to do is throw them in this small pond. The pond is not very big but it is bottomless. So once they are thrown in, the stones tied to their ankles will carry them down until they drown."

"Don't do this, Chelsea!" I said.

Chelsea said, "The decision has been made. There is no going back now." She then gave the order and both Valcor and Tabukoo were cast into the bottomless pond. They quickly went out of sight.

I then asked, "Well, is this my fate as well?"

Chelsea then said, "No, I have something else in mind for you, my friend." She then told the Wardorfs to take me to the stake of reflection.

I was taken to a large pole with a rope tied to it. The Wardorfs then tied me to the rope, strapping me to the pole. "What is this about?" I asked Chelsea.

She told me, "You are being tied to the stake of reflection. It is called this because in just a few moments you will be faced with a large monster that craves the flesh of whatever is tied to this stake. You basically will have enough time to reflect on your life before you become its meal. However, I am at least giving you a chance, unlike your two friends who are sinking to their deaths."

"A chance, thanks a lot," I said, "You are way to kind. Why don't you just kill me instead of torturing me like this?"

Chelsea said, "The way I see it is I owe you a chance after you saved my life. But know this, Abigail; don't mistake my generosity as a weakness. If somehow you survive the stake of reflection, don't cross my path again. The next time I will not show any generosity."

Chelsea then bid me a farewell and left me alone. They all exited to go free the beast from his icy prison. It wasn't but just a few moments after they were gone when I heard loud noises coming from the trees in front of me.

Out of the trees appeared the most hideous and scariest monster I could ever imagine existed. It must have been over twenty feet tall and had teeth all over its body. The monster walked up to me. I tried desperately to free myself from the stake of reflection but could not do it on my own. I had no idea what to do and had no one left to help me. All I could do was hope for one more miracle.